CRUDE

SKETCHES DONE

IN

QUICK

SUCCESSION

For Alexandra,

An outstanding reading and

CRUDE

SKETCHES DONE
IN

QUICK

SUCCESSION

a *beast* of a writer.

[stories]

Best

Andrew Brininstool

1/4/16
Tattooed Mom
Phi, PA

Queen's Ferry Press
8622 Naomi Street
Plano, TX 75024
www.queensferrypress.com

These stories originally appeared, sometimes in slightly different versions or under different titles, in the following publications:
"Kankakee" in *Five Chapters*; "Stick Figures" in *Green Mountains Review*; "Big Eyes, Wide Smiles" in *Third Coast*; "Young Arsonists in Love" in *Barrelhouse*; "Mirabeau, the Truant" in *Better: Culture & Lit*; "A World in Which None of This Shit Matters" as "The Way Lighthouses Work" in */nor* as the Editors' Prize Winner; "Horticulture" in *New Texas*; "Brass on Oak, Oak on Marble, Marble on Glass, Glass on Steel" in *Hobart*; "A Season Too Many" as "Portrait of a Backup" in *Best New American Voices 2010* and *Aethlon*.

Published 2015 by Queen's Ferry Press

Cover design by Brian Mihok

First edition January 2015

ISBN 978-1-938466-36-6

Printed in the United States of America

For Chelsea

CONTENTS

KANKAKEE

FIRST, A DUCK. It arrives in a USPS box amid packing peanuts, with Myra's address written on the shipping label. It is a mallard, its beak slightly chipped, a 60-watt bulb still screwed into the socket extending from its spine. Myra checks the label. No return address. "Oh, Jesus," she says and chuckles. A mistake. Somebody's confused grandmother. She takes the thing into the kitchen and sets it on the island. She plugs the mallard in, studies the low light reflecting off the duck's back and exposing cracks in the paint of its tail feathers. She tells herself she'll return it to the post office the next morning.

But the next morning the mailman is at her door with another package. "I'll need you to sign for this one," he tells her. It is larger than the first, and heavier. The mailman—who is handsome enough despite an outdated mustache and hair the color of old mayonnaise—struggles to keep the box in the crook of one arm while offering Myra his clipboard with the other. It is late autumn in Kankakee, much colder than it was just a month ago, but the postal worker still wears his gray shorts. Myra signs.

She moves the package to the kitchen. Inside it she finds a set of expensive knives and, underneath their block, buried deep in the packing foam, half-empty bottles of Pledge and Resolve and Goo Gone.

It goes on like this. Each morning Myra wakes and prepares for work. Just as she's getting into her car, the mail truck pulls to her curb.

9

The mailman grins. "Somebody must be sweet on you," he tells her.

She says nothing. She signs.

A paperweight with the Golden Gate Bridge suspended in the shellac. Rare collectible coins. An ashtray that reads *Jimmy Carter: A Leader for a Change*. Cookbooks. Old silk ties and ball caps with sweat-stained bills and plastic shopping bags filled with more plastic shopping bags and used votive candles and coffee tins and spoons and Black & Decker plug-in roach retractors and a set of three figurine clowns, one of which stares at Myra with green-dolloped eyes, its tongue dangling from its mouth, thumbs in its ears and hands spread wide, mocking her. *Try to catch me.*

Myra calls her mother Lucille back in New York.

"This probably happens more than you think," Lucille says. Myra's mother is always busy. She is divorced again and has decided to fill her time with the activities of a woman half her age. She goes to Bikram yoga and has her hair done regularly by a guy named Edin, a Bosnian who hacks it into elaborate dos. There are men in her life—some younger, some her age—and she has decided to take a job as a secretary at an LLC. "I never got to do the downtown working-gal thing," she told Myra after her first day.

Now, in the background, Myra hears her mother shifting papers, clicking on a keyboard. She's only half-listening. When Myra first moved to Illinois, the two spoke daily. But their conversations have become increasingly rare. Lucille is more interested in filling Myra in on gossip from the city—her voice tinged with Here's-What-You're-Missing—than listening to what is new in Kankakee.

"Just take that garbage back to the post office. They'll deal with it."

"That's the thing," Myra says. "There's no return address."

"Strange," her mother says, though Myra can tell she doesn't think it's all that strange, all that interesting a subject.

And perhaps it isn't. Perhaps Myra's life in Kankakee, only eight months in, has already become dull and tiresome—the stuff of small-town concern.

Myra works for a mortgage brokerage firm. When rumors of a transfer to the Midwest began last year, most of her colleagues had believed the new job would be in Chicago or St. Louis. When they heard otherwise, all intrigue died away.

Kankakee. Kankakee!

What an absurd name. What an absurd notion, to live in such a place.

When Myra told her mother the job came with a corner office, Lucille had said, "And a view of what? Corn? I'd rather watch a lake get dragged."

But Myra wanted the job. Things were not going well for her in the city. The Christmas beforehand, Jon, the man Myra was engaged to, had tried to kill himself. He had done it with pills ("Theatrical, don't you think?" Lucille had said), and part of his brain was damaged. "Negatively altered," according to the doctors. Myra was told it was unclear if Jon would ever recover, and to what extent he would be able to navigate the world if he did. Jon now lived in a care facility upstate; every so often he'd send a letter to Myra's mother's apartment, a sad little note written in Crayola. *I am doing just fine. The food here is just fine. The nurses here are just fine. –Jon.* Sometimes, out of nowhere, Myra finds herself sobbing, certain she is responsible, or, if not responsible, that she cannot offer enough love to stop somebody from checking into a hotel with a bottle of Celexa. When she thought of Illinois, she pictured a white-trim house she owned outright with a garden and a lawn, a new car, a dog, a local supermarket where the stockers knew what produce was ripest and shared their secrets with only her. It was a place where she could begin a new life and be happy.

And she was happy, for a while.

For a while, in the late summer, the town courted her. Myra found a nice house at the end of a quiet cul-de-sac with a backyard that gave way to fields. In September the leaves in the elms along Cobb Boulevard changed and dropped into the Kankakee River, and in the mornings or early evenings just after work Myra would jog along the Washington Street Bridge, taking in the sight: hundreds of red and yellow leaves resting on the water's surface, as if the river were ablaze. She could afford to travel now, and drove to Chicago to buy a new wardrobe, and felt no guilt on the drive back south. For the first time in her life Myra had money in savings. Her job was rewarding. Her office overlooked the quaint downtown, and farther, on the horizon, Lucille's nightmarish view of the cornfields proved awe-inspiring when sundown struck the pre-harvest just so: the red barns and silos, the bountiful yield. Myra could see her mother back east rolling her eyes; she could hear the woman saying the sight reminded her of the packaging to margarine, or Teddy, her mother's latest beau, chiming in that it was more like a glossy magazine ad for a new dick pill. For Myra in that first handful of months, it was like heaven.

"Listen, My," her mother says now, "I'm going to have to let you go. Can I call you later, sugar-bear?"

Myra tells her of course, though she knows not to expect the call.

—

When the mailman arrives the next morning, Myra decides to tell him there's been a mistake.

He frowns. "Are you Myra Gladhorn?" he asks, pronouncing her name with a deep Midwestern brogue: *Mayra Glaadhorn?* Today he wears an ushanka with the postal service eagle, but the same pair of shorts. His calves are ashy, nearly hairless except where they meet his wool socks.

"Yes," she says.

"See here," he says, running a finger across the shipping address. "Got your name, your address."

"I know," Myra says, "but the things inside aren't meant for me."

The mailman looks confused. "Uh-huh. But you see here," he says, pointing back to the label. "You're Mayra Glaadhorn. And this here is your address. You see? There's no mistake, miss. Can't be."

He leaves his finger on the box and Myra sees her name written clearer than she herself has ever written it. The mailman is right. There is no mistake. The handwriting is so careful. The 2's don't look like z's; the g's don't look like 6's. Seeing her full name written with such deliberateness is eerie, though Myra would have to admit that there's a part of her flattered by the attention to detail.

"You can file a complaint," the mailman says. "You can come down to the office, fill out a few forms. But I'd say you have a secret admirer." He grins. "Someone in North Bergen."

"North Bergen?"

"Oh-seven-oh-four-seven," he says. He shows her the smudgy black stamp on the edge of the box. "It's the postal code for North Bergen, New Jersey."

Myra signs.

"North Bergen," her mother says that evening on the phone. "Hmmm. No, I can't say I've ever known anybody from North Bergen. Charlie, that guy I saw for a while after I found out Bruce was cheating on me? He had a cousin in Passaic. I don't know if that helps. Listen, honey. You're worrying too much. Somebody has the wrong address. They're sending things to a son or daughter or—"

"No," Myra says, "this is different. For one thing, the stuff they're sending isn't normal. This morning I opened a box and found a clinical thermometer."

"Does it work?" Lucille says.

"I'm starting to worry," Myra says. There's a long pause on the line and Myra knows she's entering territory her mother is uncomfortable with—the territory of emotion.

"Sweetie, I'm not sure I can talk to you about this right now," Lucille says. "I don't know what else to tell you. I've given you my advice—what else can I do? You never listen. You never have. In fact, I'm starting to believe you actually like these mystery packages. Who knows? Who knows with you these days? You move halfway across the country, to the middle of nowhere. You call me and leave all these downer messages on my phone. Hey, I get it: I wasn't the perfect mother. But really, My. A clinical thermometer? I don't have time for this. A clinical thermometer? How is that different from a regular thermometer? Why don't you just throw it away or, I don't know, donate it? To charity? To a charity program? Myra? Hello? Sweetie? Sweetie, are you there?"

She had gone to college in Virginia, and she remembers the collective urgency and excitement that came with the news of a snowstorm. People called their parents back home. They stocked up on canned soup and Ramen in case the electricity went out. They huddled together in dorm rooms and apartments, watching the blurry pink mass on a Doppler move toward them.

For days the storm pools on the horizon. But when the snow finally arrives in Kankakee the only change in the locals is a hardening of their faces, a quiet resignation to what they've faced for centuries. Nothing shuts down. Not the schools or downtown offices. Not the factory on the north side. Not the mail.

The mailman's boots are caked with grimy ice. He doesn't bother to clean them. Instead he stands on her stoop with a broad smile and a crate the size of a child's coffin balanced on a dolly. When Myra gives him a bewildered look, all the mailman does is shrug.

"I can bring it in for you," he says.

He tracks ice through the entryway and into the living room.

"Where do you want it?" he asks.

Until now, Myra has been storing the shipped items in the guest room—the room she planned to decorate in granny-chic and toile. But the room is empty save for the boxes, which sit clustered in the middle of the floor. She doesn't want the mailman to see this, or to notice the few items she's slowly incorporated into her life: the Keurig she uses each morning to brew Earl Grey. The no-stick saucepans. The mallard lamp.

"This is fine," she tells him, and the mailman works at dislodging the cart, scraping the hardwood floor. He doesn't leave, not at first. He takes off his gloves and puts his hands on his hips and stares at the box. Something in the man's face tells Myra that he's enjoying all this.

"Want me to open it?" he asks, still grinning.

"No," she says. "I'm not sure I can do this anymore. With small things—with blenders and the like—I was willing to put up with it. This is something else entirely."

"I'll say."

Myra asks him to leave.

She waits to open the box, telling herself she won't, she's done with all of this, that the person can send whatever they damn well please and it will stay here, unopened. But after her first glass of wine with dinner—a failed attempt at succotash made in one of her new pans—Myra takes the rest of the bottle out into her backyard. She stands in the snow until her toes go numb, staring out at the wide sky and the moon. They say one can be lonelier in the city, surrounded by millions of strangers. Myra used to believe this. She no longer does. In the moonlight the snow collects in brain-gray mounds. The trees are dead. If it weren't for the fence line serrating the horizon Myra could see for a hundred miles and not catch sight of a single living creature.

It occurs to her that it doesn't matter if she opens the boxes or not. The things inside are here to wait. That's the word for it. *Wait*. These are not wayward gifts sent to the wrong address. Nor are they meant for her. These are somebody's personal belongings. This is somebody's life. Whoever it is will come for them. For it.

The box is packaged with less care, the tape striating in all directions. It takes her a while to get it open. When she does, Myra finds roofing shingles. There are hundreds of them, used and rain-worn. They come in tarred clumps, in nailed-together patterns of six or seven. The roof to a small house. Right here.

After Myra's mother divorced her father, the two moved into a cramped apartment above a dry cleaner's. Myra was ten years old. In the immediate aftermath of the separation, before Lucille met her second husband and settled down again, Lucille worked days in a pharmacy and spent her nights at a bar near the rail tracks.

Sometime around Myra's eleventh birthday, a man began to stalk her mother. His name was Lenny Chalpuski. Myra remembers seeing him only twice, though he was, for three or four months, a real presence in their lives. She recalls her mother taking long, confusing drives from restaurants back home. She recalls Lucille telling her to close all the windows and sit on the floor in the living room. There, the pair would watch television while Myra's mother braided the girl's hair, doing her best to keep the two of them preoccupied and calm.

It has been difficult for Myra to figure out just how much of a threat Lenny Chalpuski truly posed. He was a regular at the bar Lucille frequented, a drunk, but the woman continued to go there even after Lenny's fixation began. It's possible her mother had flirted with the man. Worse, she might've intentionally made him jealous of other drunks, dancing with some of them. Myra can't be certain. In those few years, Lucille became a stranger to her. Despite the late-night phone calls that ended with heavy breathing or the notes left inside their mailbox—notes her mom never let Myra look at—the woman shrugged off the attention and told her daughter, "Some people are just like that. They're desperate and don't know what to do with themselves. They don't know how to be alone."

But Myra remembers the terror. She remembers the twice-a-week occurrences when, while watching the ten o'clock news, a car would approach, its motor rumbling like thunder, the flash of its high beams cutting into the apartment's front windows. The light would settle there for a minute—though it felt much longer—and illuminate everything inside in a way that made Myra feel vulnerable and exposed. They were like people trapped in the pop of a camera bulb, people startled and frozen. And they remained that way until the car squealed off.

Just before the school year ended, Chalpuski was caught breaking into their apartment. Myra and her mother had been running errands when it happened. They came home to find two police cruisers outside. A neighbor had called. Something Myra has never told her mother is that she saw Lenny days before the incident, at the mall. She'd gone with some friends, cutting school, and spent hours loitering and shoplifting lip gloss. Then, in the food court, Myra felt a gaze on her. She turned and saw him sitting alone, drinking coffee. Their eyes met. At the time Myra had no idea who the stranger was. But she felt panic come over her.

Then the same man was in custody, glaring out from the backseat of one of the cruisers, eyeing Myra.

The ordeal was, in Myra's recollection, agonizing and sordid and long. When she was in college, Myra would find herself walking across campus late at night, or doing laundry alone in her dorm, and suddenly have an acute sensation that somebody was behind her. A man's hand reaching out, grabbing for her.

Lucille has no interest in discussing such matters. Those days are like a bad dream or an embarrassing snafu at a cocktail party. The few times Myra has brought up Lenny Chalpuski, Lucille feigns memory loss or else laughs the matter off as an essentially insignificant tidbit of history drawn large and strange in the mind of a child.

She calls her mother from work, though she vows not to mention the boxes. Since the shingles, Myra has received worthless paintings, a television, a microwave with crusted tomato soup still glommed to the glass plate tray. The items have long since spread from the spare bedroom. They have begun to crowd out her own possessions, her own life. But four days have passed without the mailman's truck pulling to her curb. Myra senses the end of the nightmare. She doesn't want to say anything. She doesn't want to jinx it.

"Teddy's brother, Kevin," Lucille says, "the wannabe novelist? He's no longer a wannabe. He sold his book. To Knopf!"

"That's fantastic," Myra says. It's Wednesday. From her office window, the hectares of corn have been harvested. They sit colorless. They look like the stubble on a dead man's cheek.

"Well, not really," Lucille says. Beyond her mother's voice, Myra hears car horns blaring, the whoosh of heavy traffic. "I mean, not for Teddy. He's actually pretty torn up about it. He's jealous. 'But you never wanted to be a writer,' I said to him last night. We were at a party. Everybody there was half our age—it was pathetic. And Teddy was drunk, really hammered. He kept going to the bathroom to inspect his bald spot. Anyway he says to me, 'Yeah, but I could've wanted to be a writer.' He's become a real downer, Myra. I think I need to end things. He believes growing older is about crossing out all the things in life you can no longer become. Those are his words."

Myra doesn't know what to say.

"Listen, My," her mother says after a deep sigh. "There's something else. I didn't want to tell you. I don't know why I am. I suppose you deserve to know. Jon is back in the city."

Her mother lets a silence hang before continuing. "I saw him yesterday. He was hailing a cab. He didn't look out of sorts or, you know, weird or anything. I'm positive it was him."

Myra considers the news. She realizes she feels nothing. "Have you considered that those packages you've been receiving are from him?"

Of course she has. She says, "Jon doesn't live in North Bergen."

"And it's impossible for anybody outside of North Bergen to send a package from there? It's a walled city, Myra? Closed off to all that aren't Bergenites? You need to call him," Lucille says. "You need to clear things up with him before he does something crazy, like mail himself." Lucille laughs.

—

She is right. Myra should call. The strangest thing she's learned in all of this—in Jon's suicide attempt, in the end to their relationship, in her decision to leave the city for a place she'd never before seen—is not how close to impossible it is to truly know somebody. No, the strangest thing Myra has learned is how easy it is to go from loving somebody to not loving them. How easy it is to fall out of love.

Because she was in love. They met during Myra's last year of college and spent every day of the next six together. He'd wanted, so often, for her to tell him she loved him, that she would always love him and would never leave. And she had done so without hesitation. In his apartment after an afternoon rain shower, or at the lodge in Vermont where they'd spent Valentine's, or while being supervised like teenagers at his parents' house in Pennsylvania. She loved him, and she'd held it as the single matter in this world of which she was most certain.

His chestnut hair. His long legs and easy gait. His melancholic eyes. Every day, Jon's traits become a little blurrier to her, a little more given over to the haze of memory. Someday, she won't remember his name.

Instead of calling, Myra spends her day at work searching Google Maps. She zooms in on North Bergen. She follows the map down one road and to the next. She eyes the pixilated street views of sad-looking houses, a meat market—pink slips of flesh visible in the windows—and cars parked along the streets. There is a man walking his dog. The Google van has taken his photograph—has sealed him inside the topography—just as he turns his head to look at the passing camera. Myra studies his half-alarmed face, the way it sags in unguarded stupidity. Is it you? she thinks.

The rest of February passes without a new shipment. March arrives. The snow begins to melt. Kankakee looks runny, morose. Myra wakes on a Tuesday and senses something about the day will be different. It's as if she knows without having to look through the window that the mail truck will be outside her house.

The package is small, smaller than the box the duck came in. She opens it on the porch, before the mailman has gone.

"What is it?" he asks.

Myra holds it up. A single brick, peach-colored and chipped.

"Anything else in there?" the mailman asks.

"No."

"I'll be damned." The mailman sighs. "Who knows? Maybe that's the end of it."

He is wrong, of course.

The brick is followed by more bricks. Pallets of them. And rolls of pink insulation. And then the beams to a house, plumbing pipes torn from the ground. Copper wiring. Strips of linoleum. When there is no more room inside Myra's house, the items begin to fill the backyard. The bricks sit on her lawn like tombstones. The tangle of copper wiring is like a bad sculpture, the metal reflecting weak sunlight. She moves her car out of the garage and, in its place, stacks the wooden beams. There is a calmness that comes with the work. Myra finds herself itemizing, checking the bricks for wear. Sometimes in the evenings she spends hours in the garage, staring at the materials, fascinated at how they come together to make a house. She is resigned to the fact that somebody has taken their life and, like a transparency on a photograph, superimposed it over hers. The feeling is not so bad, really.

The mailman, on the other hand, no longer grins. He no longer finds any of this amusing. The time he must devote to unpacking from his truck the packages addressed to Myra has surely cut into his shift. He must work harder now, Myra thinks. Faster. He looks haggard in the mornings, and unwell. Myra pictures him working overtime, returning to the main office after the sun has gone down. She sees other mail recipients giving him grief—Who gets their mail at six o'clock? What kind of service is this?—and the mailman changing out of his clothes, driving to an empty home, heating leftovers. She sees the mailman drinking too much whiskey, watching too much bad TV. He is a lonely man, she understands. Here loneliness is a state of being.

Weeks pass. Myra avoids her coworkers. She doesn't want to talk to anybody, especially her mother, whose phone calls go unanswered. They collect in Myra's voice mail. One a week. Then two. Then one a day. Lucille gives up on the cell phone and calls the landline Myra uses solely for the cable and Internet bundling package. Sometimes Myra checks the phone, only to delete messages. Sometimes, before she can hit *Delete*, she'll catch the beginning of what her mother has said. "Myra, honey, I'm worried sick—" Her mother's voice is rife with genuine concern.

There are other calls Myra is avoiding. These are from the county health services department. Myra's neighbors have complained about the lumber in her front yard, the roofing sheathing her driveway. Myra is facing fines, possible eviction. "Whatever home improvement project you have going on," she heard a man from the department say in his first message, "needs to be taken care of pronto."

Pronto. It has been nearly two months since the first brick arrived. It is May now, sunny. Around town, Myra's fellow Kankakeeites have turned sweet-natured. They spend their afternoons outdoors and linger in the dusk for as long as they can, hoping to soak in every moment of sun. Myra has hardly noticed the change in weather. In fact, on a Thursday afternoon, just before her coworkers left the office for the day, one of Myra's bosses rapped a knuckle on her office door and looked her over, his face tight with concern. "Are you feeling okay?" he'd asked her.

She shrugged. "Fine, I suppose. Why?"

He pointed at her feet. "You're wearing galoshes. And a parka."

Myra looked down at herself, then to her boss. She offered him an embarrassed smile.

—

It all ends the Sunday before Memorial Day. Myra spends the morning and part of her afternoon in bed. She doesn't get up, not even as the phone rings incessantly. She listens. Downstairs, she can hear the answering machine click on, can make out the tinny alarm in her mother's voice, though not the words.

Something has taken over her body, her mind. Her mother would call it depression. Her mother would say she has isolated herself from the world, from the people who love her. Her mother would tell her to come home, that there's a life for her yet in the city.

But it isn't depression. It's something far different, something Lucille would never understand. Maybe nobody would. If she told people that she felt as though her life had been taken over—that what used to belong to her no longer does, not even her own body, her own mind—who would believe that? Her boss? The man at health services?

Lucille would be the first in line to have Myra institutionalized; she would have Myra sent upstate, to spend the rest of her time writing fucked-up little notes in Crayola.

Here is the truth: Myra knows what she knows. She knows some energy is feeding off her—that her life has become a host for another entity, another person.

The mailman understands. It's why he arrives at Myra's house, even on his day off. When Myra answers the door, the two exchange a look, a subtle nod. The packages are now a part of his life, too.

He goes to his truck, pulls a dolly from the back. He slides a crate on top of it, secures it with straps, forces it up Myra's walkway and to her porch, then beyond her threshold. He moves the crate into the center of the room and steps away from it. He moves closer to Myra. They stand side by side, staring down at it. There is no need to wonder what's inside. It's clear to both of them. This will be the last package.

The phone rings. The answering machine clicks on, projects Lucille's voice across the house. "Myra, for the love of God. You need to call me back right this instant. Myra? Are you there, sweetie? We need to talk. This is important. Jon is here. He's here with me. He says he wants to talk to you. Myra?"

Slowly, without taking his eyes off the crate, the mailman pulls a small crowbar from his back pocket. He hands it to Myra. The tool is heavy in her palm.

A new voice echoes out of the answering machine. "Myra? It's Jon. Are you there? I have so much I want to say." He pauses. "I suppose I should start with an apology."

Myra isn't listening. She's staring at the crate, waiting for the slightest of movements.

Jon says, "I know this has been a difficult time for you. I know I can't take back what I did."

"Are you going to open it?" the mailman asks, sweat on his lips.

"Soon," Myra tells him. "Soon."

STICK FIGURES

ONCE A WEEK OR SO, when I get to feeling as if having Cody as a roommate and friend is not the wisest decision I've made, I try to remind myself of the shit he's going through and how his troubles make my own look paltry by comparison. I tell myself that behind the bravado there is a heart with a wound as aching as the man who bears it. Have some sympathy, I think, though at times—right now, for instance, as a roughneck whose name is either Jeb or Jed or perhaps simply Jeff works over my ribcage like a pro, repeatedly placing the toe of his size-11 Lucchese into a fleshy spot near my right kidney—the notion of sympathizing with Cody seems as astral as letting go of all earthly possessions to pursue Christ.

I imagine Cody could go for some of that old-fashioned Christian love about now. I can't see him—Jeb now has his hand on the back of my skull, forcing my face into the cold tile of the men's restroom floor—but from the gurgling sound coming from the stall behind me my guess is one of Jed's friends is using a belt to strangle the life out of him.

I've heard it before, the gurgling. Last weekend in fact. Cody does not like violence, not by nature. What he likes is women, and he has a penchant for indulging in this fondness with women romantically linked to men owning gnarly dispositions.

Most recently it has been Gretchen, a woman with whom Cody has had some dubious connection for the past three weeks. I met him here at Ship's after work. Ship's is a dive on a side of town so lousy it isn't even dangerous. Cody said he wanted to introduce me to the love of his life. But we had not yet finished a second round of beers when four men arrived, the burliest claiming to be sweet Gretchen's husband.

"Four," Cody had mumbled as they approached us. "That's not so bad. We've had it worse."

And quantifiably speaking, this is true. It's the quality of work this foursome has displayed tonight that is so damned impressive. These boys can dance, and though Cody and I were able to get in a few decent shots, tonight's rout has been so quick and lopsided one of our opponents has stopped to take a leak in a urinal three feet from my head, while the fourth, a little dude with a mustache whom I'd thought I could render a non-factor early but who, apparently, has some sort of extensive background in one of the more pain-inflicting genres of martial arts, is now leaning against the far wall whistling what I believe is the chorus to The Moonglows' 1954 hit single "Sincerely."

Sincerely, oh yes, sincerely...

He stops eventually, the whistler. He tells his friends enough is enough, that the police are on their way and these two ain't worth the goddamn fucking toil. I hear Cody drop to the tile, the belt released from around his jugular. He coughs for air, then lets out a heaving chuckle—a noise of gratitude, thankful for the return of oxygen to his lungs, his brain, his heart.

But this motherfucker Jeff is an overachiever. He won't be satisfied until he hears a rib crack. He keeps kicking—five and six and seven more times, each shot harder, each accompanied by a workmanlike grunt, the toe of his boot connecting with glorious exactitude—until, finally, one of his buddies pulls him away.

After they're gone, I roll over onto my back and stare up at the jaundiced ceiling tiles. For a while Cody and I are alone, breathing. Doing little else. Soon, though, I hear the door open and crane my

24

neck far enough to see Ship's eel-skin boots. "All right, knuckleheads," he says. "Get up. Get on your feet. Get out. The po-lice are down the block; I'll be damned if I lose my liquor license over this."

A few worried regulars help us to the door. We limp into the warm evening. Cody is still chuckling. I'm not. I'm beginning to tire of spending weekends needing traction. The pain in my back is such that I can't shift my car out of park and have to rely on Cody for a ride home.

We're silent for a good while. Then Cody puts in a CD he's pirated of a death metal band from Norway named The Schadenfreudes. He turns it up loud, the shot speakers in his Camry hissing.

"They killed a lamb on stage," he shouts. "A little one, like a baby or a yearling or whatever. I read about it online, in a forum. I had to translate the story into English; it was sort of hard to make out all the details, but I think they cut its head off. Then the singer, like, fucked it. On stage. In front of everybody. While he sang. He sang the rest of the set while he fucked this headless lamb. So technically that's two sins, right, Sonny? Isn't that some crazy shit?"

I tell him it is some crazy shit. My response is unenthusiastic. We've had this conversation before. I know Cody doesn't like death metal; he doesn't care for the high guitar wails or the lyrics, nearly all of which are dedicated to the Prince of Darkness and crooned through a mechanical larynx.

I met Cody a little over a year ago when he showed up at my door sweating through a cheap white dress shirt, a bike helmet catawampus on his wide head, the Book of Mormon in his hand. I'd let him in for a glass of water, and after a rather halfhearted attempt for my soul, Cody just sort of stayed. Meaning: he hasn't left since.

He traded his bicycle for a beat-up Toyota, his church tracts and dark tie for a job in the tire department at Sears. He pays for his room, buys groceries, can fix a plumbing leak without having to call the super. He swears he's happier now that his life in the Church is over and he takes full advantage of his newfound freedom by indulging in every vice our culture has to offer, approaching each new sin with the wonder of a toddler. But I know his break from the LDS isn't a clean one. I know, for instance, there's a girl in Sandpoint, Idaho, waiting for him to return from mission work—a milky blonde named Beth, Cody has told me, a girl he barely knows, a girl to whom, for certain political purposes (Cody's father is a higher-up in the deaconship) he has more or less committed himself to: he believes the marriage awaiting him at the end of his mission will bind their souls for eternity, a fate so frightening Cody is willing to do nearly anything to delay it.

And yet hell is still a very real concept to him. There have been many nights in the past fourteen months when I've sat up with him, Cody drinking my beer and telling me the atrocities awaiting him in the afterlife. And there have been times when I've wanted to tell him that's he's young (at twenty-one, Cody is a decade my junior), that he's got time to ruin his life in order to rebuild it. Yet, as I've said, mustering sympathy for Cody is a chore nearly as arduous as bending a spoon with the mind.

The music. The women. He's been calling this time of his life "The Wilderness." I'm no theologian, but I told Cody one night after he came home wearing nothing but his boxer shorts that my understanding of time spent in the Wilderness connotes a grueling, hellish stretch. "And you think I'm actually enjoying any of this?" he said.

—

The next morning I stagger into the bathroom and stand over the toilet, leaning against the wall and letting out a noise that is one-third groan, one-third chortle, one-third sob. Small blood clots wiggle like jellyfish in my voided urine. After a shower I stand for a moment in front of the mirror and inspect the Pangaea-shaped bruise forming on my side. Actually, I'm glad the bastard chose to hit me where my clothes will cover. This has not always been the case. I've shown up to work with swirling galaxies of bruised skin on my cheeks and arms; to PTA meetings with eyes cauterized shut; to Christmas parties with busted fists, knuckles the size and color of Concord grapes. Pulling on an old t-shirt and jeans, I feel confident last night's damage can stay hidden.

Cody is in the kitchen scrambling eggs.

"I'm supposed to see Callie today," I tell him. "I'll need a ride out there."

"No problem-o, chief."

"The thing is, though, if you can help it I'd rather Lorraine not see you."

Cody's grin is fixed, though he gives me a curt little nod. He keeps his eyes on the skillet. "She's still not happy with me."

"No," I say.

We leave the city a half-hour later. I've brought a pad of manila drawing paper and a box of crayons for Callie. Last summer Lorraine enrolled her in a children's arts program. I didn't understand. My idea had been to let Callie spend the summer the way I had at her age: running barefoot with a pack of other five-year-olds, poking dead things with sticks, coming home with rashes. "Times have changed," Lorraine told me. "If we want Callie to get into a good college we have to take notice of her talents and foster them now." My daughter's talent, apparently, is drawing.

Her work lines the doors of Lorraine and Paul Duncan's refrigerator. There's nothing unique about the subject matter or form. The art depicts Callie's family—Lorraine and Paul and Callie and Callie's schnauzer Ray—standing in the garden outside their home. The house is smiling—its windows eyes, its door a nose—and the sun is usually smiling too.

Sometimes my daughter will replace Paul Duncan with me, though this occurs with less frequency. Anyway, there's no real distinction between us—we are both stick figures—and save for the jagged red flame of hair on Paul's ellipsoidal skull and the drooping shit-brown on mine, we are, in essence, the same man.

You've seen something similar, I'm sure. Still I am told my daughter holds promise. When Lorraine feels pity and invites me to their Christmas parties, neighbors stand in the kitchen and stare at the refrigerator as if it were a wall to Lascaux. They roll wine in their glasses and make comments about how truly talented Callie is and how lucky we all are—the three of us—to have such a bright young mind on our hands. Once, Lorraine's neighbor Bill Johansson looked at Callie's work and grinned and told me, "Well, Sonny, I hope you have these insured. Looks like you've got a future Matisse on your hands." I told Johansson I hoped my daughter would go into market finance, that artists' lives are often sad. I told him any loving, responsible parent would want for their child a life of emotional detachment and a Roth IRA. Lorraine was not impressed; Johansson refuses to speak to me, and apparently he's given Paul and Lorraine the cold shoulder at HOA meetings. I stand by what I said. Something about my daughter being asked to explore her unique perception of reality—the jibber-jabber Lorraine and Paul and Callie's art instructor carry on about—is frightening; it frightens me to think of what she might notice, what she might choose to depict.

Soon Cody has us off the highway and whipping through hilly terrain at a speed bordering dangerous.

"Slow down," I tell him.

"What's in your bonnet?"

"There's nothing in my bonnet. I'd just prefer not to end up a pink goo spattered on the asphalt."

Cody sighs. "Okay," he says. "So it's going to be one of those days. Fine. If you want to pout and be gloomy, go right ahead. I'm sure Callie will love spending the afternoon with her sad father. But don't bring me down. I've got a lunch deal with Gretch and a good feeling in my gut. It's going to be a good day, Sonny. It's going to be a beautiful day. I feel alive today."

"Really? Because you look two weeks dead."

Cody's right eye is the blue-black of an oil spill. His throat is striped red from the belt. I know Lorraine won't be happy to see him, even for a few minutes. Aside from thinking it's abnormal for me to have opened my home to a stranger, Lorraine has made it clear she blames

Cody for my recent troubles. Just after he moved in, Lorraine allowed Callie to spend the weekend while she and Paul went to São Paulo on vacation. At the time, Cody was going around with an older woman who had him off in a bad direction. Truthfully I had no idea the pair were doing cocaine in my home. I only found out later, when Lorraine screamed at me for an hour over the phone and then demanded I drive to her house, hangdog and wretched, so she could show me Callie's renderings of the time spent with her father's new friends.

Cody runs a stoplight and turns left into the Duncans' neighborhood. Suncrest Hills hugs the rocky shores of a lake north of the city. The subdivision was built in the '70s, destroyed by a tornado, razed and redeveloped. Nothing here is older than two years: the crackless black asphalt, the one- and two-story brick homes, the Bermuda grass a green so vibrant it makes you want to cry. The only things of any substance here are fat magnolias shipped in from Mississippi to line the greenbelts and cast shade over jogging trails. It's a nice place, an exurban Shangri-la where thirty-somethings raise their young children next door to retirees. It isn't difficult to understand why Lorraine likes it here.

There is no heart-wrenching backstory concerning Lorraine and my separation—nothing worth considering for very long. We married young. I was rail-thin with some semblance of a beard and confused hair, and in the photographs from our wedding I stand straight-faced and terrified, an equally stunned-looking bride next to me.

I'd been attracted to Lorraine for her sense of humor, for her ability to see the ridiculous in any given situation, and for a sleeve of tattoos engrossing her right arm from scapula to wrist. The collected image was that of a wild honeysuckle vine, the foliage and yellow and white flowers covering the entirety of the skin to her hand. The project took years. When we first began dating the tattoo was in outline form only. Lorraine worked two jobs to save for the fill-in work.

I was with her when the last of it was completed—a small white bud on the pisiform of her wrist. We were married by then, and so many aspects of our new arrangement remained mysterious to me. All that week Lorraine had been absolutely silent; she hadn't said a single word to me. The drive to the tattoo parlor was as quiet as the late-winter rain outside.

I held her hand during the process, an act she hadn't asked for and encouraged even less. Afterward, after she'd paid and the two of us had walked out into the parking lot, the rain heavier now, the sky rolling onto itself in low sooty puffs, Lorraine told me she was pregnant.

For two years we managed to make something of a life together. The simple truth is that Lorraine managed to shift hers in a way I never learned to, and on an October afternoon when my mother had offered to look over Callie so Lorraine and I could spend a day together, the two of us went to a nearby restaurant for lunch, the plan being to grab something light and a Bloody Mary (Lorraine) and a quick beer (me) before heading to the mall for some shopping. The lunch lasted almost five hours. Our first drinks turned into sixths, sevenths, and by the end of it—and here I can't even begin to chart the trajectory of our conversation—we somehow broached and answered a number of questions that'd become part of the undercurrent of tension within our marriage. Lorraine asked me, for instance, if I enjoyed being a father. And I told her that I loved Callie dearly and that I'd do anything for her. But, no. Truthfully, I didn't care much for fatherhood. And I asked her if, when she imagined our future, she saw us living in a large house in a quiet neighborhood and, as a follow-up to that question, if she felt that we—her imagined duplicates of ourselves—had made our decision based at least in part on the merits of nearby school districts. She answered yes to both. She asked what my plans were concerning a career (I had none) and I asked her to list what she wanted most from life (she couldn't), and by the time the bill came and we parsed together enough cash to cover it and leave a lousy tip and get up from our booth and stagger out, dazzlingly drunk, into the cold afternoon, our marriage was over. I drove us back to our apartment and we made love. Then Lorraine brewed coffee and we sat in bed a while and watched an old movie on TV and sobered up. Lorraine drove to my mother's to pick up Callie. The two of them moved out a week later.

And a year after that, Lorraine met Paul Duncan, a consultant for TransAtlantica Airlines, and moved to Suncrest Hills.

I was happy for her and for Callie, and happy Paul wasn't an insufferable pain in the ass. (In fact, Paul and I used to play racquetball before a bad lumbar sidelined his game.) It is not, all things considered, the worst outcome. Still, on days such as this one, on warm Saturdays when I'm sore both in body and spirit, I can't help but visualize myself in Paul Duncan's place and the sheer joy that must come to him when, say, grilling steaks in his roomy backyard on a hot summer evening, or golfing with a levelheaded pal, or falling asleep next to a wife who's as beautiful as she is apneic.

But the chasm between Paul Duncan and me is a wide one, and in the end it seems only cosmically just for Paul to have what he has and for me to go around with a marauding Mormon in exile.

I am thinking about all of this when Cody parks at the Duncans' curb. Lorraine is already outside, waiting. It's the first time I've seen her in months. Over time her tattoo had become only noticeable to me when pointed out by a stranger. It was a part of her, no different than her brown eyes or how her right knee was home to dozens of pale freckles. But this past winter, when she told me she'd begun laser removal treatments, something in me cracked. I got hot with her, shouting things I hadn't known I felt and calling her names I'd never called her before. The rage in me was frightening and unexpected. While my vision didn't go red my voice took on a castrato timbre, the words entering the receiver tiny and bound together. Lorraine shouted back, saying I was attempting to control her body, to own her. I told her to cut the Intro to Fem Studies shit, that the matter at hand concerned her inability to commit to anything long-term, her irresponsible attitude toward all things in her life—an argument I still don't buy. I'm not sure what overtook me that day. What I do know is that things between us haven't been good since.

But in the midday sun, Lorraine looks like a vision of near-perfect creation. She wears a sundress so sheer you can make out the gentle curvature of her hips. Her hair is cropped and auburn, and the sight of her leaves me dry-mouthed and joyous. The feeling doesn't last. Lorraine gives me a long stare before turning her gaze on Cody.

"Hi, Lorrie," he says. "Kick-ass spread you got out here. I'm digging the hydrangeas."

"You both look like hell," she says. And then to Cody: "What are you doing here?"

"We had a minor car accident last night," I tell her in hopes of explaining the welts and bruises on Cody's face and neck. "Mine's been towed. I needed a ride."

"I'm just dropping him off," Cody says, turning toward his car. "Not staying. Plenty of things to do today."

"Right," Lorraine says. It's difficult not to look at her arm, not to ogle the gray fog of ink, the places on her wrist and mid-forearm where the honeysuckle and green vines melt away. "Like converting unbelievers by sleeping on their couches and bringing home stray cokeheads."

Cody looks hurt, but he offers a smile. He says to me, "Give a ring when you need me to come get you."

Lorraine and I watch Cody fold himself back into his small car and drive away from the house, death metal shaking the Camry's frame. After he leaves I follow Lorraine inside.

I've been to the Duncans' more often than I can count, but it's still a strange feeling walking into the airy front rooms of the house, standing in another man's domain.

"Where's Paul?" I ask.

"L.A."

"Again?"

"Still. He's been there all week. They can't reach an agreement on the peanuts *vee* pretzel debate. He should be back Monday."

An obnoxious sing-along blares from the television, but I don't see Callie. As if sensing what I'm about to say Lorraine tells me, "She's taking a nap. I'll go wake her."

A while later Callie appears at the top of the stairs. Her hair is tangled; her eyes are puffy from sleep.

"She's a bit of a grouch after her naps," Lorraine says.

"Hey there, Callie-co," I say, pulling the drawing pad and crayons out of the bag. "I've got something for you."

Her eyes light up some, but she doesn't look as thrilled as I'd hoped. She nears me and looks over the gifts. I take the opportunity to pick her up in my arms and squeeze her tight. She lets out a shrill yelp. "Put me down put me down put me down put me down."

"She doesn't like to be held," Lorraine informs me. "It makes her feel like a baby."

I put Callie down. I ask her, "Where do you want to go today? The park?"

"The park is stupid," she says.

"The park is stupid?"

She nods.

Lorraine says, "Paul's been taking her there a lot recently. I think she's a little burned out. Also, there's a girl from the neighborhood who patrols the slide like a gatekeeper."

"What about the lake?" I suggest. "We could feed some ducks. Lorraine, do you have any bread we can take?"

Lorraine finds a half-empty bag of sandwich bread and tells me to be careful. Callie and I cut through the Duncans' front yard and down the street to a place where a thin gravel trail weaves through sumac and live oak before fattening into a maintenance road. The road moves down to the shores of the lake. I've brought Callie's drawing supplies and carry them in one hand; Callie holds the other and kicks rocks as we go.

It's a little after three when we reach the small crags overlooking the lake. Below us sits a pebble beach, and I put Callie on my shoulders and struggle down the embankment. Callie wraps her arms tightly around my neck. Her sandal digs into the bruise on my side.

On the shore, I unbuckle her shoes and take off my own and roll my jeans. The two of us wade into the warm water. It isn't long before an old man in a johnboat putters by. He waves. Callie and I wave back. A slight wake rocks a pair of boathouses a hundred or so yards to the east. Callie and I throw rocks at the water. Truth be told, the beach is not as lovely as it had looked from above. A sizeable hornet's nest dangles from the soffit of one of the boathouses; the hornets weave threatening patterns in the air. And I have to remind Callie to watch where she steps: in the shallows just off the beach dozens of tiny things glisten like coins plopped into a fountain—blades and treble hooks from discarded fishing lures.

Also, there are no ducks, not so far as I can see. But Callie and I have fun anyway. We spend our time tossing bits of bread into the water. Most of the crumbs flatten out and go soggy before sinking, but every now and then a small perch will appear just below the surface, eyeing a clump for a few seconds before striking. Callie is riveted.

My phone buzzes with a text from Cody: *its ovr w gretch.*

I text him back. *Should hope so.*

Crushed, he writes back. *Nevr felt so bad. n despair.*

I'm in the process of replying when I hear Callie let out a shriek. She's a hundred or so yards to the west, squatting low over the beach. I sprint toward her, fearing she's stepped on a rusty hook. But what she has found is a gar, fully grown and washed ashore, swaying with the light tide. It's newly dead from the smell, and its awful toothy mouth looks like a lawn-care device for a pasture in hell. Callie's own mouth hangs open. She has one finger outstretched, ready to prod its scales.

"It's a *monster!*" she cries.

"Don't touch," I say.

The two of us stand there a moment more. Instantly I recall a morning fishing with my father two decades before, when I was nine or ten years old. He'd caught one accidentally, his large crankbait buried in the animal's gills. The creature thrashed at the side of the boat, its bony head thudding against the aluminum hull, its mouth open and aimed at my father's hairless knuckles as he tried to free it. Eventually my old man had to cut his line. The gar disappeared into the water, the hook still deeply embedded.

—

Soon the sun drops and I take Callie back up the embankment. We find a concrete picnic table in a small park overlooking a wider section of the lake. Callie tells me she wants to draw. I give her the pad and crayons and she goes to work. I try not to interrupt. I want to talk to her. I want to ask her about her friends and how she likes school. Her tongue hangs out of her mouth.

Eventually the light dies on us, and I have just enough time before dark to look over her drawings. The first three are what I expect: simple depictions of me and Callie standing in the water; me and Callie waving to a round, smiling head in a boxy boat; me and Callie and a fish. But on the fourth sheet Callie has drawn the gar. The animal stands on its fin, vertically, surrounded by blank space—no beach or rocks or water, nothing but the creature we saw a few hours earlier. What's strange are the details. Callie has attempted to draw the gar accurately; unlike the pictures of us—various lines and circles pushed together to create a rendition vaguely human—my daughter has paid attention to the creature's scales, its long beak of teeth, its dark, dead eyes. A full-bodied image. An attempt at depicting life the way it truly is—the details important. It's the first I've seen her do.

All the lights are on at the Duncan house and from the street the place looks as if it is leaning dangerously toward us. I find Lorraine in the kitchen, and near the refrigerator Paul Duncan stands with his arms on the marble island, a bottle of beer next to him.

"Paul," I say, shocked to see him.

"Hey, Sonny," he says and smiles. It's been a while since I've seen him. I'm startled by the changes. His hair, which had once been thick coils of fire, is now thinning, turning a flaxen gray. He looks gaunt and tired, his clothes wrinkled from the flight. Paul sees Callie and squats down, pulling a bag of airplane peanuts from his pocket. "I've got something for you," he says. Callie goes over to him. She takes the bag in her hands, struggles to tear it open.

Then Paul takes the drawing pad and begins to flip through it. "Negotiations broke down," he tells me, though I haven't asked. "They sent me home early. We're meeting at Dulles next week. Jesus. It's been nine years. You'd think in nine years we would've figured out how to pull our heads out of our you-know-whatsies."

He stops on the picture of the gar. I wait for him to say something, to point out the scales and fins, the minor details Callie's worked into the depiction. Instead Paul scrunches up his nose.

"It's a monster," Callie tells him.

"It's a gar," I say.

"Lovely," Paul says. "Introducing our daughter to the joys and wonders of deceased aquatic life, Sonny?"

"Maybe you could hang it on the fridge, Paul," I tell him.

"It'd certainly add something."

"Christ," Lorraine says, joining Paul. "This is something she saw?"

I nod.

"Funny," Paul says. "Somehow I still have a good appetite. You're staying for dinner, Sonny?"

"Probably shouldn't."

"It's almost ready," Lorraine says.

Paul stretches his back and lets out a yawn that becomes a groan. "Good," he says.

Over salmon kabobs and quinoa, Paul talks about his job, about the effects of September Eleventh, about a new system one of TransAtlantica's competitors is considering: pay-for-use johns. "Can you imagine some poor fool standing outside one of those tiny airplane lavatories shoving crinkled ones into a cash slot, nearly pissing himself?" He speaks without looking at Lorraine or me, instead staring glumly at his plate. He interrupts himself only long enough to move to the refrigerator for another beer. Callie has a cut-up hotdog on her paper plate, a lake of mustard to the side. She hums to herself.

After dinner, Callie falls asleep face-planted on the living room sofa, her bum aimed at the ceiling. I have a quick chance to say goodnight before Lorraine takes her upstairs. Paul and I do the dishes.

Then Paul says, "Grab a beer. Come outside with me."

I text Cody to head toward Suncrest Hills. Outside the night is still muggy, frogs audible from the lake. Paul leans over the porch railing, his head cocked slightly toward the sky.

"What makes you happy, Sonny?" he asks me after a moment.

"Happy." I don't know Paul as one with a penchant for searching questions.

"Yeah," he says. "What makes, you know, Sonny Campbell a happy guy?"

I shrug. "Don't know what to say to that, Paul. Are you all right?" I ask, hoping his answer is yes, hoping my ex-wife's husband doesn't want a shoulder to cry on.

"What I am is tired," he says. "Lorraine says I get to travel across the country while she has to stay in the burbs. I try to tell her what I do isn't traveling. What I do," he says, drinking beer, "is sit in conference rooms for eighteen hours a day listening to old men with ulcers bitch about overhead costs, then go back to a twin-bed room and order a seventeen dollar hamburger." Paul finishes his beer and says, "When I told Lorraine I had to go to D.C., she said she wanted to come. It's impossible, though. Callie has her classes. School starts soon."

"I could watch her."

Paul looks at me. He shrugs. "That might be an idea. I'll have to run it by Lorraine. She's still not happy about last time."

I try to quell any excitement, but my heart turns like a dually engine.

I've come to understand that Cody is new to the highs and lows of Eros and therefore crushed every time a tryst falls apart. On the drive back to Ship's, Cody is as bad as I've seen him. "I meant what I told you," he says. "About her being the love of my life." Highway lights strafe through the car. Cody looks at me, waiting for a response. When I offer none he says: "You don't believe me."

"It's more that I hope you're joking."

"What is that supposed to mean, Sonny?"

"You'll have to forgive me. I'm sitting here with my fingers crossed, hoping somebody hasn't turned my car into a public toilet.

And I'm eighty percent certain I'm suffering acute renal failure. If you're telling me the love of your life—the reason I need to contact my primary care physician—is because you fell in love with a buck-toothed girl from Deer Park, well, I might just toss myself from the car right now."

"Hey, fuck you," Cody says. His voice goes high when he curses, the words still dangerous artillery. "Watch what you say, asshole."

A while later Cody says, "Look. I'm sorry. I am. I've put you through a lot of shit."

"Don't worry about it."

"No, Sonny," he says. "You've been a good friend. In many ways, you've upheld the tenets of Christianity better than I have."

I give him a look. "I thought you'd dropped that piety stuff."

He's quiet for a moment. Then, in a voice so low I hardly hear him, Cody says, "Beth called today."

"What'd she say?" I ask.

He shrugs. "I didn't answer."

"Voice mail?"

"Yeah. I haven't checked it."

Cody exits and pulls into Ship's parking lot. I'm lucky; my car is still parked where I left it last night. "Whatever she has to say I've already made a decision," Cody says, pulling up beside my car. "A big one. I'm going celibate."

"Like a priest?"

"Sort of," Cody says. Then, "No. Not like a priest at all. Just celibate. I'm through with love. It hurts too much."

Cody's celibacy lasts roughly four days. On Thursday evening he comes home from work with a sizeable bolt pierced through his right eyebrow, the skin around it swollen and red. He stops at the condo only long enough to clean grease from beneath his fingernails and change clothes and cologne himself and quickly fill a Hefty bag with some boxer shorts and socks and jeans and a toothbrush. He stops for a moment in the kitchen, guzzling from a carton of grape juice. "I'm getting a tattoo," he tells me, slinging the trash bag over his shoulder. "Me and Alexis—we're driving to Reno. And we're getting matching tattoos."

"Who's Alexis?" I ask.

Cody laughs. "Who's Alexis? What a question!" He offers a bewildered grin and a look that seems to say, *Oh-my-god-can-you-believe-what-stupid-shit-I-get-myself-into?*

Just before he goes, Cody gives me a long, constricting hug. "You're a good man," he says. "A good person with a good soul."

I ask him if he's saying goodbye.

"We'll see," he says.

Lorraine calls the same night. She tells me she and Paul have talked it over; they think it's not such a bad idea for Callie to spend the weekend with her father.

"We're flying to Dulles tomorrow night," she says. "It's short notice, I know."

"It isn't a problem."

"We'll be back—*I'll* be back—Sunday afternoon. Short notice. Short trip. I hope that's okay."

"Absolutely," I tell her, doing my best not to sound too elated.

I spend the rest of the night cleaning. I vacuum and dump the Folgers can Cody was using as an ashtray. I clean toilets. I pull the refrigerator away from the wall and do battle with a large culture of mold growing on the tile. That night, I find myself unable to sleep. With my eyes closed, my brain fills with a hodgepodge of meaningless but frightening images. Awake, I can't help remembering Lorraine. How she once looked. How, on the afternoon the final bud was filled in, her arm looked bizarre and pretty and out of place in a world gone gray with winter.

What makes you happy? Paul wants to know. I'd like to tell him it was that day; it was standing in the rain, your wife, Paul, turning to me, the skin near her wrist pink and glossy with Vaseline, her words—I'm pregnant—breaking a glacial shelf that'd somehow formed between us when we weren't paying attention. But I know this to be a lie. I know that in that moment I felt only terror and confusion, and what makes me happy is the memory of that moment and not the moment itself.

—

They show up later than expected, Callie already asleep. Paul takes her into my bedroom. "She's eaten dinner," Lorraine tells me. "In all likelihood, she'll sleep through the night. There's a chance she'll wake up—midnight or so—and want to be read a story. I've packed some books in her bag."

Paul emerges and checks his watch, says, "Plane leaves in an hour. You'd think the man entrusted with their future business model would get special treatment, but I've got to stand in my socks and have a pat-down just like the hoi polloi."

The three of us walk down to the parking lot. The night is oddly cool, a respite from eighty-degree evenings. Paul is telling Lorraine to make sure it's Terminal B and not C because it's a pain in the ass to get back out onto the main thoroughfare, and Lorraine is telling Paul she's certain it's B—she checked it twice before they left the house—when a man staggers up the drive.

His body is mostly shadow in the haloes of the lot's lights. At first I mistake him for an out-of-breath jogger or one of my many divorcee neighbors. But it becomes apparent the man isn't out for a stroll. He cuts between Paul's BMW and the three of us. Then he is near me, near enough that I can smell rye on his breath. He looks up at the apartment, then says: "Eight-one-three Henderson."

"I'm sorry?"

"This eight-one-three Henderson? You Cody Gaffe?"

He's perhaps sixty, with muttonchops and a blue-and-yellow pearl-snap shirt untucked from a pair of Wranglers. He sways close to me, then away, like a sapling in rough weather.

"Sonny?" Paul says. He has his keys out and hits a button on the pad. The headlights blink twice.

"I don't know what you're talking about," I tell the man.

"Bullshit." He points to the apartment. "This is eight-one-three Henderson, and you're the son of a bitch thinks he's going to run off with my daughter." The man pulls a wad of paper from his pocket and holds it up long enough that I can tell something's been written in a looping, girlish hand, but not long enough to make any sense of it.

"Sonny," Paul says again. "What's going on here?"

"And who're you?" the man says to Paul.

"Do you know this guy?" Lorraine asks.

"No," I say. "He's just some drunk. Come on. You need to catch your flight."

I move to Paul and Lorraine and try to usher them to the car. But the man stumbles toward us and puts his hand around my elbow. "That ain't happening," he says. "Nobody's going to Reno."

"Reno?" Lorraine says.

"Who's going to Reno?" Paul says.

"*He's* going to Reno," the man says, jabbing a finger into my chest.

"What?" Lorraine says. "When?"

"I'm not going to Reno," I say. "I'm not going anywhere."

"Goddamn right about that," the man says. "You ain't going anywhere. Not with my daughter." He looks at Lorraine. "She's sixteen, goddammit," he says, his voice choked. He tries to push the note to Lorraine, but I grab his wrist and bring his arm down to his side. The man leans into me. I shove him back and begin to tell Lorraine about this, about Cody and Reno and the girl, Alexis. But the man bows his shoulders. I know what's about to happen.

Maybe it's all those weekends with Cody that've made me keen to the nearly indiscernible particulars of an oncoming fist. The quick intake of air. The tightening of the lips. The way the eyes go dull and half-closed, like a cat pouncing at a bird. Whatever the reason, I know the punch is coming before the old man cocks his arm, and so it takes nothing to sidestep his attempt, to watch him unfurl his small body like a snake. I hear his fist meet something and when I turn I see Paul clutching his eye with one hand, the other still extending the keys. A stupid, pained look on his face. The effort takes a lot out of the old man; it's no difficult task to force him to the ground, to put my knees to his bony chest, to keep him there.

"You bastard," he mutters. "Let me up."

"Rest," I tell him. "The cops are on their way."

He tries a few jerking movements; in truth there's no real effort. The anger has left him. He looks tired now, sad.

The police take our stories without attempting to conceal their boredom. They ask Paul if he cares to press charges. Paul says he isn't interested in any of that. He just wants to go home, he says. The cops arrest the old man for public intoxication. Lorraine says she's going to wake Callie. Paul follows her. I stay outside a moment more, watching the police put the old man in the back of their cruiser. When they leave, he looks out through the back window at me, his eyes heavy with tears.

Upstairs I find Paul sitting on my sofa, a Ziploc bag filled with ice pressed against the side of his face. With his other hand he holds a cell phone to his ear and talks to a ticket agent about rescheduling. Callie is in her pajamas by his side, her head in his lap. So often Paul pins the phone with his shoulder and runs his fingers through Callie's hair.

"Unbelievable," I say to Lorraine, who's sitting at the cheap kitchen table Cody and I went halves on a few months ago. She has her legs out in front of her, her elbows on her knees. She won't look at me. "Isn't that just unbelievable?" I say. "I don't know how else to describe it. Maybe now you see why I'm trying to move out of this place."

Paul tosses his phone on the couch. "I was able to reschedule my ticket for tomorrow morning. No such luck with yours, Lorraine. Who knows? Maybe next week—" Paul doesn't finish his sentence.

"Jesus, Paul," I say. "I'm really sorry about all of this."

Paul doesn't say anything. Neither does Lorraine, though eventually, after what seems like an eternity, she looks at me. It isn't a look of anger or disappointment. I'm used to those. This one is something colder than that—a look one stranger gives another on a crowded bus.

A while later, just before they leave, Paul asks me for a hand mirror. I rummage through the bathroom and find one and bring it out to him. He places the bag of ice on the coffee table and holds the mirror up to his face. We all crowd around him as if expecting to see something hideous. Instead we see his bottom eyelid has turned pink; his eyebrow floats down a slide of puffy skin toward his retina.

"It's not so bad," I tell him.

Paul lets out an aggravated chuckle. "Yeah?" he says. "And how am I supposed to explain this at the board meeting?"

"You're hurt," Callie says.

"No, sweetie," Paul says. "I'm fine. See? I'm fine." He leans in close to her and lets her run a finger along the tender skin around the wound. Her mouth hangs open, her eyes steadfast on Paul Duncan's face.

"Don't push it," Paul tells her. "Just look."

And this is an image I know I'll remember for a long time, long after Cody gets dumped in Reno and heads back to Idaho; long after Paul's eye heals; long after the ink on Lorraine's arm has disappeared: my ex-wife's husband sitting on my sofa with my daughter's fingers prodding his face, mapping all the places it differs from mine.

BIG EYES, WIDE SMILES

MISS OKLAHOMA IS ALL BOUND UP AND SNARLING, the ball-gag in her mouth slick with saliva. "Gurrghl-rugh!" she says. "Gurrghl-rugh!" But Ron isn't in the mood. The drive from Tulsa took nearly eight hours and his back is killing him. And while he might be willing to admit that these past twelve days have been thrilling, *exhilarating*, he's beginning to doubt whether leaving his wife and daughters and shacking up with a dethroned beauty queen whose thirst for sex and pain cannot be quenched hasn't proven to be somewhat of a mistake.

Twelve days ago in Idabel, under a blood sky, they first met in the dimly lit bar of a historic hotel; the couple spent that night in Ron's suite entering into positions both foreign and elaborate. The next evening Ron found himself in Muskogee, in a Super 8 so close to the highway the sheetrock vibrated when semis passed and, where, in the throes of passion, Miss Oklahoma used her incisors to open the flesh of his lower lip. In Norman, whips. In Wetumka, Ron came to understand the intricacies of horse bridles, the metallic aftertaste of the bit. This jaunt across Miss Oklahoma's native state has been as frenzied as their nights together, moving Ron toward a feeling of chaotic glee, and this morning in Tulsa, when she told him it was time for her to leave the state, Ron agreed to take her, certain their passion was enough to fuel them all the way to California.

But they've yet to cross the state line, and when Miss Oklahoma sees his desire falter, then, quite literally, go slack, she sighs and works herself into a more natural sitting position. With measured grace, she slips her svelte wrists from the handcuffs, uncoils the leather straps from around her breasts, and removes the gag, placing it, Ron can't help but notice, with disappointment in her lap.

"I'm just a little tired," he says.

She pats his thigh. "It happens."

"You and my wife should start an It-Happens Club." The comment is biting. He regrets making it almost immediately. Gina Crenshaw, which is Miss Oklahoma's legal name, gets up from the bed, pulls on her robe and, looking around their tiny digs—from the old black-and-white in the corner to the gold-spackled mirror hanging crooked on the wall to the little hotplate on top of the bureau—lets out a bereaved moan. She is tall, redheaded, with a broad angelic face. She is twenty years Ron's junior, a fact that has bothered him only peripherally until now. The truth is they have nothing in common, no reason for being here together. When they first began, it wasn't so difficult for Ron to imagine otherwise. It wasn't difficult to imagine them as rightful companions. They are both running.

Currently, Gina is on the lam from the Oklahoma Commission for Beautification and Image Promotion, a committee of nine stern men who oversee the pageant every year. They've put the word out for Gina Crenshaw, who owes them back their sash and tiara and who is obliged, as they see it, to offer the rest of the Sooner State a heartfelt apology for tarnishing the reputation of their province. Ron isn't from here, but he's been in the state long enough to have ascertained a few key details surrounding the imbroglio. He knows that Gina spent last spring involved in an ongoing tryst with one of Tulsa's leading news weathermen, a man also nearly twice her age. Ron knows the sex between them was complicated and masochistic in part because he, too, has had such relations with the queen, and in part because (and here is the crux of the uproar) these assignations were in fact videotaped.

Eight tapes, spanning nearly twelve hours, showing the lithe Miss Oklahoma and the varicose-veined meteorologist entering into brands of coition the likes of which most human beings will never experience—certainly not at this longitude. The tapes were stolen from the weatherman's home and uploaded to various Internet sites. Sometime last month, while Ron was still back in Charlotte, the meteorologist gave a teary-eyed apology to his fellow statesmen from his front lawn, a silent and very peeved-looking wife by his side. He acknowledged that he'd let down the people of his fair burg, who'd come to rely on his forecasts. He claimed to be entering into counseling and said he only hoped to regain their trust.

Why Gina hasn't done something similar—why she has instead absconded, refusing to give back her crown—is something Ron has yet to understand. Nor does he plan to ask. He knows the weight of ruin firsthand, the subtle intricacies of a person attempting to escape the mess of their own life.

In North Carolina, Ron has made a successful career for himself as a maxillofacial surgeon, an occupation initially born from high intention. There was a time when he saw himself correcting the cleft palates of Appalachian schoolchildren and restoring the noses and ears of burn victims—righting all of God's cruel mishaps. At some point, though, Ron found himself married and the father to two children, saddled with a mortgage he couldn't afford. Soon he lost the saintly pretense and resorted to working out the minor kinks in women of financial substance. His abilities are well-known and respected; he's been paid handsomely for them. In Charlotte, Ron has a house built of solid pine, energy-efficient windows, a spare room with a sixty-inch television, a boat slip, fifty-one percent ownership in a time-share in Vail. In Charlotte, Ron has two daughters growing into long skeletal structures. In Charlotte, Ron is known for his Kennedy hair, his drinking problem only slight, his handicap at the country club a cool sixteen.

Last year, after receiving accolades as *Preeminent Facial Reconstructor of the South*, Ron spent no small sum on a car, an Aston Martin, a little V-

12 that can tear the limbs off saplings if he revs the engine just so. Outside Bungalow Six, beneath a dying sun casting pale light, the Aston's green paint job, described by the dealer as "regal," looks to Ron more of a sickly, meconium hue. So this is it, Ron thinks, watching Gina apply lip gloss in the tilted mirror. This is getting old.

Quickly, then, comes the panic, the fear that Gina knows this, knows that he is simply another unhappily married man, a dick on its last outing. To quell it he says: "Let's do something tonight. Let's get out. Have dinner. Some drinks."

Gina snorts, a noise he's come to learn means *You don't know shit about Oklahoma, Ron.* "In case you've forgotten," she says, "we're in Umpstead. In the panhandle. Quite literally the middle of nowhere." Soon, though, she slides into the bathroom and locks the door, and he can hear her getting ready.

Those evenings on the prairie. The way the sun glints off the Indiangrass. The world here goes forever in all directions. The sight of such brings on euphoria, an immense appreciation for the largeness of things, and, Ron has felt, gives meaning to your place within it. But too soon the plains give way to the rocky, alien terrain of the panhandle. In the lushness of the state's midsection, Ron thought he was saving Gina, and that she was doing the same for him. Against a new backdrop, in a territory lacking fecundity, their lot looks so very different.

Earlier this afternoon, while Gina snored quietly in the passenger seat, Ron looked out off the highway and saw a memory from his boyhood materialize: a series of brief-stay bungalows made from stucco, buildings as round as uncooked dinner rolls and painted sherbet green. Taken together, the structure is meant to resemble a long dragon or lake monster, its benevolent creature-head (the office) adorned with childlike eyes and a wide smile suggesting encouragement of one's travels. Ron saw it in the distance, just as he had nearly forty years ago: the dragon looking poised for the Pacific, like them, its large vertebrae cresting a sea of golden prairie.

He'd all but forgotten his family's stay in Umpstead. The sight of the lodge brought on a flood of nostalgia. He'd been nine then, the trip West his father's final gift to Ron's mother. After her diagnosis, the old man had saved what he could and planned the family's excursions to the Grand Canyon, the Four Corners, the Hoover Dam. Less than a week after school had let out they loaded the station wagon's roof with suitcases and duffel bags. Two weeks later, on their way back to Charlotte, they stopped in Umpstead and rented a bungalow.

He woke Gina. "Let's stop there."

She adjusted her eyes, looked out at the motel, then to Ron. "You're joking."

Ron clutched her hand and eased them off the highway. He didn't tell her about his family's trip—the parameters of their relationship, so far as Ron can tell, don't allow for discussions about dying mothers. "It'll be fun," he said. "A bit of kitsch to remember your home state by."

He tried to keep this same attitude even as it became apparent the motel wasn't what he remembered it to be. The grass is high and overcome by two-foot stalks of ragweed. An obsolete TV satellite nearly the size of a city block sits alone to the south, buckshot holes in its dish, the feedhorn dangling from its center like a snapped bone. Ron and Gina's bungalow, Unit Six, stands near the tail end. After they'd received their room key the couple walked through the courtyard, passing the swimming pool where Ron recalled spending an entire day in his childhood with his brother Mark, the two of them chasing each other around the pool's edge and doing cannonballs into its cool water. The pungent tang of chlorine came to Ron quickly, culled from memory, and from memory alone: the pool before him this afternoon was a pit half-filled with water the color of tea, home to beer cans and discarded Pampers.

Ron noticed a man kneeling at the far end of the pool. He had his arm forced into a drainage pump. The man looked up. Ron waved. As a return gesture, the stranger gave him a slight neck-bob and pulled his hand from the filter: clutched in his grip was a drowned nutria nearly the size of a football; it dangled from his yellow kitchen glove like a distended, sopping hairpiece.

But Gina's libido is a marvel. No sooner had Ron shut the door to Number Six than she was out of her clothes and digging into her purse for their goodies. "This place looks like it hasn't seen any action since Reagan was shot," she said, dumping a string of festively colored anal beads onto the floral-print duvet. "Let's bring the walls down."

Ron, still anesthetized by memory, felt his lower back with his hands.

Now he walks to the front office to ask the woman who runs the motel for a dinner recommendation. She is a tiny shriveled thing behind smudged plexiglas, her attention on a romance novel with a library ID taped to its spine. Ron waits. When he and Gina checked in, Ron had considered telling the lady of his stay at the lodge as a boy. But she'd given Gina a disapproving eye, and whatever Midwestern Howdy-and-Thanks Politeness he'd expected was nowhere to be found. Taped to the divider, alongside a list of fraudulent check writers, is a handmade note: DO NOT TAP ON GLASS. The curt interaction from earlier leaves Ron worrisome of what the lady might do if he were to violate the glass-tapping rule, and so he finds himself resorting to jangling the change in his pockets. The woman puts her novel down. "I see you," she says. "I've been seeing you. Couldn't wait for me to finish my chapter, huh?"

"Sorry," Ron says.

"If this is about the hot water, you'll need to talk to Dennis. Dennis handles those things. He's in Unit Nine—the tail."

"No," Ron says. "The hot water is fine, I think." He gives the lady the friendliest smile he can muster, the look he gives a woman before putting her under and taking a scalpel to her face. "I was wondering what you'd tell two lovebirds who want nothing more than to have a large time on the town."

"I'd tell them they're S.O.L."

"Nothing?"

"There's the VFW Hall on Eighth Street." The woman re-opens her book.

"I was thinking something a little more intimate," Ron says. "Somewhere we could get a nice meal. Wine, maybe."

"Wine," the woman says, chuckling. "Honey, you're in a dry county. Looking for wine here would be like looking for a spare prick at a couples' retreat."

—

"I want to see how cruel the world is," Gina told Ron a few days ago. "How ugly it can be. Isn't it weird, Ron, how we can fake beauty, how we can try to hide what's hideous, but it always seems to find its way to the surface again?" They were in Stillwater, lying on the twin bed of a TravelBright Lodge, the afternoon sun coming through the blinds and striping their nude bodies.

"I hadn't thought of that," Ron told her, though he had, many times.

"I was four when my mother began entering me in pageants. Formal wear, swimsuits, makeup. Big eyes, wide smiles. Hours in front of mirrors with curlers in my hair. She quit her job, my mother. Quit my father. Took me from one town to the next. We lived with relatives, with some of her former boyfriends. They never touched me, by the way. I feel the need to say that. When I won, Mother'd take me to Tastee Freez for a hamburger. Then it was on to the next town. I saw all of Oklahoma that way."

"What about when you lost?"

"You think I lost?" She rolled onto her stomach and pulled a pack of Camel cigarettes off the nightstand and lit one. "Here's the truth, Ron. My childhood was a happy one. How many people can say that anymore?"

Ron did not reply. Gina was thinking. She said, "The question, the one they always ask that really gets me is: What is one change you'd like to see take place in this world during your lifetime?"

"I'd like to hear your answer."

"'I would like to see cultural ignorance, racial and gender inequalities and religious bigotry eradicated; that humans will come to view the differences among us as miniscule and worth celebrating; that we are, in essence, a tribe, with a collective heart and a desire for joy and equanimity.'"

"That sounds like more than one change."

"Do you know how many times I've said that? Do you know what I've always wanted to say? I've always wanted to tell them that I wish the world would peel back its rind and show us its vile, pulpy inner-heart."

Ron waited for Gina Crenshaw to explain her answer. He studied the curvature of her spine, the pale freckles just beneath the shelf of her buttocks. She pulled a final drag and turned her head quickly. "You're about to kiss me on the ass now, aren't you, Ron?"

"I was considering it."

"Come here, you big man," Gina said, and put her cigarette out on his elbow.

Miss Oklahoma has left bruises. His ribs ache. His haunches are striped with bubbling welts. Yet every time she emerges from the bathroom donning a different disguise—a long, platinum blonde wig; contact lenses that turn her eyes sea-green; painted-on freckles—he feels his heart tighten and dive, like a duck shot out of the sky.

The feeling returns as he hustles back through the courtyard, the backache receding, a heavy yearning welling inside. He wants to tell Gina that they're checking out, crossing the state line pronto, gunning the Aston across New Mexico and Arizona and not stopping until they smell brine in the air. But at twenty yards, Ron sees that the door to Unit Six is open. He hears laughter. Gina's high wail, and, along with it, a guttural chugging, like a tractor engine trying to turn over.

Inside Ron finds the man from this afternoon standing at the far end of the room, hands in the pockets of his cut-offs. Gina, who is lounging on the bed, looks over. "Hi, Ron," she says. "This here is Dennis."

The man offers his hand. Ron is reluctant to take it, remembering the rat-in-the-pool incident. "Pleasure," Dennis says once they do finally shake. He looks at Ron with deep-set gray eyes. His hair is tight coils of sun-stained blond, and he would not be ugly if it weren't for a mound of scar tissue over his right nostril, a lump of skin that makes the organ look more like a charred piece of Tupperware than a nose.

"Denny was just telling me some things," Gina says.

"Funny things, it sounded like," Ron says.

Dennis says, "Just a few corny jokes I've heard along the way."

Gina has put on a wig—this one jet-black, a kind of Twiggy bob—and her eyebrows are penciled in thickly. A fake mole is glued near her bright red lips. This is not one of her better disguises. She looks, Ron thinks, in many respects, like a transvestite. There is something else different about her, something beyond the disguise. A sharpness to her eyes, a coldness in the way she looks at him now. "Ron isn't much up for jokes, Dennis," Gina says, her grin curdling. "Ron isn't much up for much."

Before Ron has time to form a response, Dennis says, "Unit Six," looking at the ceiling, the small bureau. "I'm sorry for this. I told Na-Na to put you in Four. Four's been remodeled. Six is a mess."

"You do the maintenance around here?" Ron asks.

"Maintenance, groundskeeping, renovation, painting, carpet installation, plumbing. Sometimes the books, too, when Na-Na loses her glasses or else a little more of her mind. I wouldn't say loping around an old motel with my grandmother is my idea of a good life. There's something a little Norman Bates about it." Gina laughs, a bit too earnestly. "But this place is my inheritance. I'm hoping to get it ready to sell. Soon as the old woman kicks it, I'm in escrow." Dennis smiles when he mentions the possibility of selling the place, but Ron finds all of this depressing—a man waiting for his kin to die before he feels he has the right to leave. Dennis looks at Ron and asks, "What is it you do?"

"I'm a surgeon."

Gina says, "He fixes faces. He tries to change ugly." If the comment bothers Dennis, if it makes him self-conscious about his nose, he doesn't show it. "But you can't change ugly, Ron." A strand of her red hair has come loose from beneath the wig, and she's wrapped a thin finger around it. "It does you no good to try."

"Anyway," she says to Ron, "you're being rude. You've interrupted Dennis here. He was about to tell me some more things, some things about prison."

"Prison," Ron says.

"Denny served time."

"It was a long time ago," Dennis says.

"It sounds like the two of you have covered quite a bit of ground this evening."

"Didn't mean to interfere," Dennis says.

"We have," Gina says. "We've talked about just about everything."

"The hot water?" Ron asks.

"Is it not working?" Dennis asks.

Ron sits on the edge of the bed, sighs. "It's fine. But there's nowhere in town to go for a drink. Gina, I think we should probably get back on the road. We can be in Santa Fe if—"

"I don't think so, Ron. I don't think I want to ride in your car anymore today. And besides, I thought your back hurt."

"Back trouble?" Dennis asks. "I've got Ibuprofen in my room."

"What'd be good is a stiff drink, something Umpstead is apparently unwilling to offer."

"I've got that, too," Dennis says. "Follow me."

Unit Nine, the tail, Dennis tells them, used to be a cocktail lounge. "Totally illegal. But the old man figured if he was going to charge adults to stay in a place that looks like a jungle gym the least he could do was offer somewhere to come after their kids were asleep."

Dennis tells them he's in the process of renovation, and Ron must stop himself from saying, "The early stages, it looks like." A cot is set up in the corner. Alongside it, a small lamp, its red glass shade reading *Winston tastes good like a cigarette should!* Aside from a sodium bulb above the old bar, the lamp offers the only light in the room. The walls are in need of a paint job, and there is a persistent smell to the place, the tang of a room locked for years. Altogether, Ron thinks Dennis's little hideaway has all the cozy ambiance of a sepulcher.

"It isn't much," Dennis says without irony.

"It's snug!" Gina says.

Their host grabs some old stools, places them around the bar. Then he pulls out a bottle of Teacher's and a bottle of Old Crow. "Like I said, this used to be a neat little place back when." He pulls a half-empty bag of ice from an arrhythmically humming mini-fridge and grabs three glasses from a shelf. "Of course, the old man got caught. Had to close up this room. Lost his lodging license for a while. That's when the property started going to pot. When he died," Dennis says, pouring whiskey over ice, "the place was all he had to give to Na-Na."

Ron looks around. He can see it, the way the room once must've looked. Briefly he lets himself wonder if, after he and Mark had gone to bed, their parents snuck into this space, had met here with other adults on their own treks across the hinterlands. He knows such an event never occurred, that his father, a Baptist, had hated bars and alcohol, and by the time his family made it to Oklahoma Ron's mother was so sick she barely stayed awake past seven o'clock. Her hair was gone then, and her skin had turned sallow. Still, for a moment, Ron allows himself to believe the false memory. He sees his mother healthy, drinking wine, laughing, allowing her husband to take her by the hand and, embarrassingly, out into the middle of the lounge—roughly where Dennis's third-hand sofa sits. He pictures his parents here, the two of them enjoying themselves in a way they never truly did.

Dennis pours another drink. Gina asks him what he went to prison for, then asks if it's a rude question. "Simple curiosity," he says. "Anyhow, the way I see it, a girl sharing a drink with a man she hardly knows in an old motel on the edge of nowhere has a right to be given a basic rundown of the felonies he's committed."

Then Dennis says, "But it ain't an interesting story, I'll warn you."

"Don't be modest," Gina says, smiling and moving closer to him, the way she had with Ron in Idabel after he'd mentioned the things he'd seen in surgery.

"A meth deal gone wrong. I was selling shit my cousin cooked up. Got caught with a pound of it in my trunk, and took off when the trooper tried to pull me over. They followed me for fifty miles before they broke out the spike-strips. I flipped the car off into a ditch."

"Is that what happened to your nose?" Gina asks.

Dennis touches the place where his nostril is missing. "No," he says. "That happened later."

After more prying on Gina's part, he tells them the story. According to Dennis, he got in wrong at the joint, offering a cigarette connection—his cousin—to an Aryan group. But after a close encounter with one of the guards, Dennis's cousin no longer felt safe smuggling cartons inside, and when Dennis relayed this news to the group one of its members took a handmade cauterizing tool to his face. "You can still see the hairlike wisps from the end of the copper wiring," Dennis tells them and tilts his head back. "In many ways, I have Norton G. Blassingame to thank. His assault led to my parole. But one of the many mind-fuckingly shitty qualifications of my deal is that I can't leave the state for another three years. I've got to check in with this asshole, Dwight, over in Boise City every two weeks."

The three finish the Teacher's, begin to share the Old Crow straight from the bottle. Soon Ron knows he's drunk, can feel it in his cheeks and ears. Ron finds himself admiring Dennis's candidness, his sincerity. When the bottle comes back to him, he takes a long pull, then hears himself say: "I stopped here with my family, years ago. I was nine, I think. We were on our way back to Charlotte from the Carlsbad Caverns. My mother was sick and my father had decided to show her all the splendor of the American West while she still had the chance to see it."

Gina looks at him, surprised. "What was she sick with?"

"Ondigliocarcinoma."

"What's that?"

"Cancer."

"I don't know what to say, Ron," Gina says. "Did she like it?"

"Cancer?"

"No, dummy. The splendor, or whatever you called it."

Ron considers. "I think we went looking for splendor and found snake pits, fake turquoise jewelry. Motels meant to look like sea creatures."

Dennis finishes a drink. "It's a kind of splendor, I suppose."

There is more Ron can tell them, like how his father spent the trip frustrated and underwhelmed, angry that the land did not offer its bounties in the unspoiled condition the old man's mind had anticipated. This hadn't come as a surprise to Ron, who knew his father spent most of his life leery that the world had him pegged as a mark. He could not enjoy so much as a nice summer evening, Ron recalls, without feeling as if it came with a price tag, a cost, whatever it may have been, that was fifteen percent higher than honest.

In Lincoln County, New Mexico, for instance, Ron remembers his father screaming at him and Mark because the boys wouldn't let up on wanting authentic deputy badges from the Billy the Kid Ice Cream Saloon and Gift Shop. "They're ten bucks each," he'd told them, his face reddening. "Ten bucks for a lead star you boys'll lose just as soon as you take it off."

Sometime that afternoon, at a point when Ron's father snuck away to bum a cigarette from a fellow tourist, Ron's mother took the two boys into the saloon and spent some of her own money on malts. She also bought the badges, telling her sons, "You'll have to hide them until we get home. Can you do that? Can you put them in your suitcases and not take them out? Promise me."

They had, though ultimately the old man was proven right. Before they'd made it back to Charlotte, Ron had lost his badge, and Mark, so far as Ron knows, had lost his, too.

—

Just as they've finished the bottle of Old Crow, the bulb over the bar flickers. A loud clap of thunder shakes the walls.

"Spring thunderstorm," Dennis says. "Been happening damn near every week. They get bad here. Some nights you can look up and see the entire sky turned white from lightning. All you'll see is bolts dancing and spreading for miles, one right after the other. And not a drop of rain." A look comes over Dennis's face. "You have a car," he says. "I know a place. I mean, there's something I could show you."

"It's a coupe," Ron says. But soon enough the three are standing in the parking lot, Ron fumbling for his keys. Dennis looks over the Aston Martin, says, "Maybe there's room behind the seats."

"Nonsense," Gina says. "You sit first. I'll ride in your lap."

He directs Ron out onto the highway, then down a farm-to-market road. They pass a burger joint and eventually level out onto the main strip, a boulevard where old shoe stores and pharmacies and a Western wear place lean against one another. They follow this road until it ends. "Turn left," Dennis says, and soon they're pulling away from town, past the small high school and a nursing home, nothing illuminating the night sky but the unsystematic blue-gold tines of lightning.

They nod along on a gravel trail. Then, it seems, no road at all: a divoted patch of hard clay, the shocks on the coupe doing all they can to keep up with the ever-increasing roughness of the path beneath. They crest a hill and Dennis says, "Stop here." Ron and Gina follow him up a rocky path to the head of a tall crag. Dennis finds a boulder to sit on. He puts his arms on his knees and looks out over the valley. The lightning turns the dome of the sky into fractured glass; the strikes stay just behind Ron's retinas a few seconds after they've passed, like echoes, like the memories of things you've loved and forgotten. This, Ron thinks, was what his father had wanted to show his mother. This was what they'd missed that first time. Jagged crags and arroyos running like dried veins and, beyond all of that, nothing but space, *land*, as red as Martian soil and so free and open it feels impossibly stupid to think you're really ever moving toward some end point, some finality. Ron can't tell how long they stay there—how long they take in the warm electric air—but all too soon Dennis stands and makes for the car. "We better get back on concrete before the hill turns to mud."

But Dennis was right the first time. There is no rain, just the threat of it, the low and quick clouds and lightning strobing across the plains. The drive back to the motel is so quiet Ron jumps when Gina first speaks. "They're here," she says in a near whisper. Then, louder: "They're here. Christ, Ron. They're here!"

Beneath the googly eyes of the main office, a state trooper's rig is parked alongside a white pickup. The search for Gina is something Ron has nearly forgotten, and the sight of the cars takes from him any tranquility he'd felt at the crags. He cuts his headlights, coasts the Aston Martin to the back of the motel.

Gina is in a panic. "I've got to grab my shit," she says. "I've got to get out of here. Like, now. Like, come on, Ron." But something happens to Ron. When he tries to picture himself in California, he sees Dennis there instead. He sees Dennis relaxing on the beach, taking sun on his neck and cheeks and on the cold dead swath on his face. Here is Dennis, worry-free, unchained by his birthright and the guarantee that comes with it, the promise that if he stays here he'll never leave.

Ron takes the keys out of the ignition and, reaching over his shoulder, drops them into Dennis's lap. "The plates are out of state," he says. Dennis looks down, confused.

"Ron?" Gina says. "Have you lost your fucking mind?"

"Don't stop," Ron says to Dennis, then to Gina. "No matter how tired you get."

"Ron," Gina says again. But he is out of the car, moving beneath the crackling sky toward Bungalow Six.

There is enough time to hide the sash and tiara under the bed, but a knock at the door comes before he's had a chance to deal with Gina's toys.

The two men from the Commission take their time. They look around the room agog, unable to hide their disgust. The state trooper picks up one of Gina's non-rigids—a tangerine-colored device known as the Drillbit—and holds it at arm's-length, allowing the toy to flop some, like a dying bass. "And these, sir," he says, dropping the toy back onto the bedspread, "*all* of these are yours?"

"What is life," Ron says, "without variety?"

One of the men from the Commission gets down on his knees and sweeps a hand underneath the bed. He says, "Here we are, boys," and pulls out the tiara, holding it in his calloused hand.

After that there is a lot of nervous movement. Some calls are made. Ron spends time in handcuffs. Then he's released to sit on the bed. The men from the Commission drink coffee. The young cop goes at his braces with a floss pick. Finally it's decided—by who, Ron can't tell—that charges won't be pressed, that they'll ask him to stay in Oklahoma for a few more days, take a deposition, and let him go. "You'll be home free," one of them says.

After they leave, Ron locks the door, brushes his teeth, changes out of his clothes and slides into bed. The storm has picked up. Ron had imagined the units here to be made of reinforced concrete and heavy rebar—built like pillboxes. But that's not so. Each time thunder claps, the room quakes as if attempting to uproot itself and flee.

Sleep doesn't come easy. Ron knows that in the morning he'll call Charlotte; he'll talk to his wife. What he'll say to her is another matter. He doesn't know if he wants to go home. Returning means facing the pain he's caused, the rift he can never repair. It's clear to him now that he doesn't know why he left in the first place.

The night drags on. Ron lies in the dark, listening to the world collapse around him. So often he thinks, *I'm dead.* But when he opens his eyes he knows he isn't. He prays the storm will flood the whole world, will wash all of it away.

But in the morning, Ron feels perfectly fine. He wakes to the sound of a mower, loud beyond the thin walls of his bungalow. He pulls on Gina's robe and makes coffee with the room's little hotplate.

Then Ron goes out onto Unit Six's small porch and leans his arms over the railing and sips his coffee and watches: out in the field beyond the motel, less than one hundred yards away, Dennis is pushing a red lawnmower through the thick tangle of weeds. So often the engine lets out a gurgling noise and chokes quiet, a quick puff of diesel exhaust rising when Dennis raises the front end and lets disembodied milkweed stems fall from beneath the blades; once cleared, the blades whir back to life. For a second, Ron wants to look over at the parking lot and see his car, gleaming in the morning sun, Gina leaning against it—both the Aston and Miss Oklahoma waiting for him. He doesn't look. He knows the lot is empty. He knows these weeks have been a costly illusion.

Dennis pushes the mower in a wide arch through the brush toward Unit Six. The sky is an opulent blue. The wind carries the scent of cut grass. Dennis makes it halfway across the field and stops, killing the engine. Ron watches him walk out beyond it and stare at the ground. Crouching like a child, he digs his fingers into the soil. Then Dennis stands, holding something in his palm. He looks back to the mower, then to Unit Six. He puts his eyes on Ron. The wind dies away. Ron waves and, in response, Dennis raises his hand high above his head, palm outward, fingers clasped around something old.

YOUNG ARSONISTS
IN LOVE

CONSIDER THIS FAIR WARNING: you aren't going to like me. If the last four decades of business luncheons, casual encounters, tête-à-tête's, romantic and platonic minglings, marriages and divorces, Memorial Day barbecues and Christmas parties and doctor-patient and lawyer-client and produce-manager/produce-consumer exchanges hold true, you won't be able to stomach me long enough to finish this story. I've come to grips with my deficiencies, though it took the better part of my time here to realize that life doesn't unfurl its graces to each of us in complete and tidy bundles. Maybe you don't get the woman you love, or a face that pleases a stranger's gaze, or the strong heart and sturdy bones to get you through; maybe you aren't granted a disposition that leaves others feeling safe and giddy in your company. But you do get something. I've been given the moral compass of a tyrant, with twice the wealth.

Ten years ago, I made a fortune off a potty-training device called Daily Constitutionals. At its heart the contraption is little more than a tricked-up training seat coupled with a six-inch LCD flat-screen monitor from which an animated little girl with big green eyes and pigtails asks a series of multiple choice questions concerning the

U.S. Constitution, the legislative and judicial branches—basic Western civ. The machine comes equipped with voice-recognition software developed to understand and interpret baby talk—everything from advanced babbling to full-sentence chatter. State-of-the art sensors, designed by a tech company in Baden-Württemberg, are embedded in the sides of the bowl. Anytime stool or a stream of urine is detected, the child is rewarded with a series of new questions. I'm forty-one now. While it's become clear I'll never have a child of my own, if I did I'm not altogether certain I'd want the little sport learning his right to bear arms while in the middle of a tee-tee.

Still, there have been enough parents with imaginings of their little mewlers becoming the next Ruth Bader Ginsburg to keep Daily Constitutionals marketable. The residuals are such that I'll never have to work again. And this, according to my former wife Sheila, is the worst thing that could've happened to a man like Gordon Gephardt.

We met while I was still relevant on the baby-genius circuit, pitching my product to children's chain stores. Sheila was a sales rep for InfantCo. We were introduced at a convention in Tacoma where I'd been asked to give the keynote address on the long-term viability of the micturition/maturation market. "Anal Retention," I was calling the speech. Not the greatest joke, but one that had Sheila bewitched that night at the hotel bar.

In retrospect, I can tell you that we were drawn to each other by our mutual disdain for all things generative—namely, parents. Young parents. The ones who'd yet to see clearly the scourge their loins had foisted upon civilization. We detested their sentimentality, their fear, their naiveté—the qualities on which we'd each advanced our careers. That night in Tacoma, over a fourth round of drinks, Sheila and I agreed that the best thing one could do on behalf of humanity was to avoid procreation. And it was on this single pillar of mutual misanthropy that we decided, five months later, to construct a marriage.

Sheila, as I've mentioned, is no longer in the picture. If you were to ask her, the dissolution of our relationship stemmed primarily from my drinking. Without anything to occupy my time, Sheila will tell anybody who is willing to listen, her voice deadened by years of therapy-speak, that I allowed myself to devolve into a man-child, a walking id whose sole purpose was to indulge in whatever pleasures were immediately at hand, thus wreaking emotional havoc on those who truly loved and cared about me. The devil makes work for idle hands, she will say, and since the release of Daily Constitutionals mine have been as idle as a mop on a slaughterhouse floor.

I don't necessarily disagree with Sheila and her head doctors. Recently, in fact, I've taken steps to curtail my intake. I still drink, but nowadays I've made a pact with myself: for every rye I down I owe a mile on the jogging trail. The system might not be a cardiologist's wet dream, and it's no fun to pass a pretty young woman while smelling like a creature long-deceased, but it suits me all the same.

So it was two autumns ago when I was entering my fifth mile, still drunk but sobering, whiskey leaking from my pores in thick, odoriferous waves. The trail near my house meandered past pee-wee soccer fields and out beside a small pond before doglegging back toward an enormous wooden playground shaped to look like a castle. That evening, I'd looped the pond and was heading back toward the playground when my leg began to cramp. I was winded, knocking along at little more than a trot. The sun had gone down, the last blaze of evening sitting just beyond a grove of pecan trees. I stopped at a bench and ran my shirt over my face and tried to knead some of the cramping from my calf. When I looked up I happened to see, just beyond the freakish shadows the castle's spires cast against the trail, movement from within the curtain walls.

I wandered over the faux drawbridge and into the large center, where seesaws and make-believe knights' horses constructed out of old tires sat in a large square of sawdust. For a moment I saw nothing; then, at the far edge of the playground, two small figures hunched in a corner. Lost children, I thought.

But when I came upon them I knew they weren't children. They

65

weren't lost. Two teenage boys, both in dark, baggy sweatshirts, squatted in the corner. Almost immediately I smelled gasoline. For an instant I envisioned the sight from a distance. The gatehouse and towers swallowed by flames. A medieval horror here in exurbia. It was an astonishing thing to imagine.

One of the boys turned and locked eyes with me. It took him a while to nudge his friend, the boy applying fuel in a crooked line along the beams of the east wall. I expected them to run. They stayed put, pinned to the spot by fear. I felt the same—this was my first interaction with budding arsonists—but said to the boys, in the most authoritative voice I could muster, "Put down the can. Slowly."

The kid did as he was told. It was darker now, what was left of dusk diving behind the houses to the west. The boys waited, not knowing what would happen next. I didn't know either, not until I found myself saying, "Come with me."

I marched them into my neighborhood, led them down the hill to where my house sat at the end of a barren cul-de-sac. Sheila and I had purchased this property in part because it was far from the city and miles from the nearest neighbor. The house still sat on its own block, though recently strangers had purchased the lots around it; now neat squares of razed land flanked the property and pallets of plywood sat ominously, like tombstones for long-dead giants.

The house had once been moderate in size, but in a twelvemonth of mania, Sheila and I had added rooms, empty spaces we had no need for or intention to use, so that the place was now a sixty-five hundred square foot monument to grief with all the charm of an end-times compound.

I took the boys into the foyer, which, after seeing a photograph of Franz Ferdinand's Konopiště, I'd had decorated floor-to-ceiling with the horns of animals I was too cowardly to kill myself. The pair were agog, taking it in. I interrupted, asking to see their driver's licenses. The boys quickly looked to the floor.

"You don't have licenses?" I asked. I looked at the boys for the first time in the light and realized how young they were. One had the spongy cheeks of an infant, the other, a sharp chin speckled with down, a stud in his ear. "You aren't old enough to drive."

They said nothing.

"Ages," I barked.

"Fourteen," said one.

"Thirteen," said the other. "But I'm practically fourteen."

"Wallets?"

They dug into their pockets and produced identical leather tri-folds, probably stolen. I sifted through each, finding the contents of inchoate adulthood: a membership card to a place called GamerZone; three wrinkled dollar bills; a condom so old the label had worn off its flinty packaging. In one, I found a 2x4 photograph of a blonde girl. A yearbook photo. The girl's awkward smile bore braces, and her hair rose from her skull teased and AquaNetted like a sand dune held together by industrial waste.

I held it out. "Who's this?"

"Give it back," the taller boy said, childishly, as if I intended to hold it over his head and make him grab for it.

"That's Rebecca," said the shorter one. "She's Kyle's girlfriend."

"Shut up," Kyle said, his face flushed.

"It's her birthday tomorrow." He grinned.

"Rebecca's?" I asked.

"Shut up, Stephen."

"That's what we were doing at the playground. He was gonna impress her by burning it."

"Shut the fuck up, Stephen. Jesus."

"I'm glad to see the mating rituals of the young have advanced since the Stone Age," I said. After I said it, a strange thought struck me. I realized these two boys had likely taken their first grown-up shits on a throne of my creation. Or, if not these two, certainly scores of their generational counterparts. It wasn't a good feeling to understand that I might've played a role—no matter how slight—in their choosing to lay ruin a public recreation facility in hopes of copping a feel with a hairspray addict. Here, then, was the end result of Daily Constitutionals manifested before me: two glabrous and confused boys, as horny for destruction as they were for nookie.

Eventually, I found their library cards. Kyle Birchmier. Stephen Goad. I put the cards in my pocket and said, "Do you like movies?" They stared at me. "Go in there," I said, "into the living room. Bottom two drawers of the entertainment armoire—there're thousands of DVDs. Pick one; I don't care which. Put it on and raise the volume as high as you like. Doesn't matter. Go nuts. I'm going to shower. If you're gone when I get back, I'm calling the police."

"Dude, this isn't some weird perv thing, is it?" Kyle asked. "You're not gonna like come out of the shower all naked and shit, asking us to soap up your junk?"

"Yeah," Stephen said. "We heard about that shit at school."

"Do I look like a pervert?"

They shrugged.

"Go," I said.

They shuffled into the living room, letting their breaths out when they saw the size of the television. "DVDs," I yelled again, "are in the bottom two drawers."

Soon I heard the roar of the speakers, the rumpf of the subwoofer. I made my way outside and to the guest house where, since Sheila's leaving, I'd more or less secluded myself. It was painful to be in the house for any considerable amount of time, painful to roam the hallways and rooms Sheila and I had once occupied.

We'd been married a little more than three years, and there'd been a mistake. It's not a period of time I like to dwell upon, so I'll simply say this: after Sheila told me, I spent a few hours wild, smashing things both expensive and cheap, pitter-pattering from one room to the next with my fists clenched. I asked her if it was truly a difficult task to take the same goddamn pill at the same time every day—if it required a degree from the Sorbonne. In turn, Sheila made *lingchi* of my ego; she pointed out that our sex life was as frequent as a lunar landing. We cursed each other and fell into silent bouts.

I was raised Catholic, and one evening over dinner I informed

Sheila that while I no longer believed in most of the tired verities, I couldn't bring myself to violate a few of them. Sheila, who was slurping up the noodles of her chow mein, gave me a smile so filled with hatred I've yet to see it duplicated by any living creature. "Fuck you, Gordon," she said. "I've already decided to keep it. Your involvement from here on is strictly academic."

Something strange happened over the next few weeks. I would call it a process of conversion, though that would make it sound histrionic. Still, I began to see my life in new terms. I came to grips with the idea of being a father. I daresay I began to look forward it. One morning Sheila and I broke our silence with each other. We had a talk, and our lives, we decided, now looked re-routed toward if not sunnier pastures then certainly land we could occupy and graze contentedly together. We began Lamaze classes and read books. I called a contractor and had a nursery built onto the east side of the house. Sheila and I began to consider possible names. We agreed on a boy's, Troy, because it was simple, strong. But one afternoon Sheila said, "If it's a girl, I want to name her Josephine."

I looked at her. "My God. It's hideous."

"It was my mother's name."

"That poor woman."

Sheila crossed her arms. She told me she wouldn't consider an alternative. I let the matter rest, hoping to revisit it when the time came. We never got the chance. A couple of days later, Sheila lost the pregnancy.

The grief that followed was, in my estimation, the fait accompli to our marriage. Sheila began therapy, a course of action that would prove helpful. Eventually she was able to pull herself out of the cave of agony and became, quite honestly, a person I no longer knew. She began yoga, bought whole-hog into the-power-of-positive-thinking hokum. I attended only a few sessions, found them ineffective, limp-dicked. What I needed were nails, concrete. Copper wiring. Grout. I needed projects, the expansion of something permanent and tangible. And when the sun set and the roofing contractors and drywall technicians retired for the day, the only thing left to quell my soul was a rye over ice.

—

I found the boys sitting on the leather sofa, captivated by a movie in which things blow up.

"Good," I said. "You can follow directions." The boys ignored me. "Come on," I told them. "I want to show you a few things."

I took them through the kitchen and down into the basement, which I'd had converted into a game room: vintage pinball machines, a billiards table, darts. Then we went upstairs to the library and back down again, past the parlor and formal dining area and out into the backyard where I showed them the heated pool and Jacuzzi. We went out to the wine cellar, an addition I'd paid handsomely—and happily— for. I showed them bottles of Côte de Brouilly and Meursault. At each stop, I listed off dimensions and upgrades—the marble inlay of the foyer, the granite countertops in the kitchen, the different grains of redwood used for the crown molding—as if I were showing the home to potential buyers.

We ended up back in the kitchen. "All the appliances are new," I told them, opening the refrigerator and taking out a can of beer. "They're stainless steel. The cellar holds over five hundred bottles, and there's a stocked bar in the game room. I had security cameras installed last winter; there's a channel on the television: you can watch the north end of the property, the driveway and backyard, all without missing a single minute of *Who Wants to Marry the Tyrant of a Small, Tropical Nation-State?*" I took a long pull from the beer. "What do you think?" I asked. "You like?"

Stephen Goad said, "This place is badass. How deep's the pool?"

"Twelve feet."

"Awesome."

"Yeah," Birchmier said, giving me a smart-ass little grin. "It's all right. But I'm not in the market."

"And I'm not selling," I told him. "Listen," I said. "I've got to go out of town for a day or so. I want you boys to look over the place. You know: housesit. Have whatever you want from the fridge. Watch movies. Play video games. Bring girls over. Throw a bacchanal. It's all yours. Then, I want you to burn it to the ground."

The boys looked at each other.

"Ah, come on," I said. "We're not losing our balls now, are we? Think of how impressed Rebecca will be once you set alight sixty-five hundred square feet. I'm getting keyed up just thinking about it."

The two young wannabes were now looking very much their ages, very much like boys who wanted to go home to their parents.

"I don't know," Kyle finally said.

"I'll throw in a grand apiece. You know, for college funds." I finished off the beer. "Listen, boys. If anything goes wrong, I'll take the blame. One hundred percent of it."

I told the pair to think it over. If they wanted the gig, they could come by the next morning and shake on it. "And if not, no sweat. Buy Rebecca a friendship bracelet and leave conflagrations to the pros."

They left soon after. I took the other five beers and a quilt out onto the back porch. From there I could see, just beyond what remained of the woods, a thin finger of a lake a quarter-mile to the north, flashing cold and gray in the night. In the summers Sheila and I had often come to this same spot, nude, lounging like housecats, feeling as if the world had cracked its hard shell and offered us, just us, its contented meat.

I fell asleep in a lounger that night. In the morning, Kyle and Stephen were at my door.

I left town the same afternoon. I was going out to Lloyd Kissinger's blueberry farm, where Sheila now lived. She'd met Kissinger under similar circumstances as she had me. Lloyd was the author of a series of books—*Your Child, at Five*, *Your Child, at Ten*, *Your Child, in College*, etc.—that claimed to present how parenting decisions affected future lifestyle and behavioral choices. Most insiders viewed him as a fraud, but Kissinger had a top-notch agent and had once appeared on a leather sofa across from Oprah; in the immediate aftermath of the show, parents across the country rushed to buy his brand of ersatz psychology. I couldn't bring myself to hate Lloyd for his success. I could for fucking my wife.

Kissinger was immensely tall and thin, emaciated from a diet of wheat germ and legume casseroles he felt certain would keep him alive into perpetuity. Considerably older, he wore sensible Rockports and his longish hair brilliantined into a ski slope. His goatee hung without an accompanying mustache. Of course, I, too, was tall and older than Sheila. And I had my own facial hair misfortunes (a beard I'd committed myself to in my late twenties, despite its patchy growth). And while booze had bloated my midsection and cheeks, when Sheila met me in Tacoma, I weighed barely one-seventy. Nonetheless, I felt incredulous rage that my wife had chosen to copulate with a man who closely resembled a praying mantis crossbred with C. Everett Koop.

I was traveling to Kissinger's under the pretense of a missing prototype for a new product I'd been half-assing into creation for nearly seven years. Somewhere deep inside, though, I knew I simply wanted to see Sheila. And this admission, this understanding that I still felt dependent upon her, connected to her, was discomfiting. I'd pulled a Riesling from the cellar, and somewhere on Highway 117, unable to overcome the unease, I found myself holding the bottle between my thighs, the cork on the passenger seat. I roared on, shifting gears when necessary, listening to the crack and hiss of a Cardinals game broadcast on a lousy AM signal.

Kissinger's spread hugged a hilly acreage in the country. Dozens of rows of blueberries grew on the west side of the longest slope and down throughout the short valley. In the spring and summer they gave the landscape a cool violet hue. In the fall the trellises sat naked, like rows of unused crucifixes awaiting the condemned.

I pulled up the long drive and parked. Nobody was home. I waited. An hour passed. The afternoon waned. I took a few more swigs from the Riesling bottle and finally made my way to Kissinger's garage. I typed 1-1-1-9 (b-a-b-y) on the keypad. The door opened.

Kissinger's house was airy, with big rooms and vaulted ceilings and enormous windows overlooking a pond in his backyard. His bookshelves held thickly spined history biographies and were littered with small woodcarvings, trinkets he'd amassed from vacations to distant, poverty-stricken nations. His furniture was expensive. But his television was an old Sanyo with a three-click remote. I turned it on and leaned back into a chair, not bothering to take off my loafers before settling my legs on an ottoman. Another hour passed. I finished off the wine and fell asleep.

I woke to the sound of voices on the front stoop. The light in the room had shifted. It was dark now. I heard the deadbolt unlock. Sheila came in. She carried grocery bags and had her head craned, saying something behind her to Lloyd. When she finally saw me she stopped for a moment, though soon she fixed herself. It wasn't entirely unsurprising, I suppose, for her to see that her ex-husband had broken into her lover's house.

Sheila looked around comically. "Where's the duct tape?" she asked. "The blunt object for the backs of our skulls?"

"I brought wine," I said, handing Lloyd the empty bottle.

He looked it over, then smiled and extended his hand. "It's been a while, friend."

"We're friends?"

"How'd you get in?" Sheila asked. She turned to Kissinger. "Shit, Lloyd," she said. "Did you forget the alarm again?"

Lloyd waved her off. "Those things make me uncomfortable. We're putting in a gate. We're setting alarms. We're placing surveillance cameras in trees. What kind of life is this?"

"The cameras are a good idea," I told him.

Lloyd glanced me over. "You look good."

"Right," I said. "And you look young."

Lloyd winked, something he did all too often with me, as if we were in on the same grand joke. While Kissinger had always been accommodating and willing to put up with my impromptu visits, I knew there was more to him, that he wasn't the kind guru he wished to appear to be. Before Sheila, Kissinger had been married to a woman named Dianne. The ins and outs of Lloyd's first marriage, and the bizarre and grotesque way in which it ended, had become common knowledge among the infant-product circles in which we both ran.

As the story goes, Dianne had been a gorgeous young woman, though at some point during the marriage she'd begun to lose her mind. There is the famous tale of the time Dianne had remarked to one of her and Lloyd's neighbors that they (the two women) didn't see enough of each other and that Dianne would love for the woman to stop by one afternoon for coffee. When the woman took Dianne up on the invitation, knocking on the Kissingers' door, meeting a frazzled and out-of-it Dianne at the threshold and explaining that she'd come by for that cup of coffee, Dianne had left the woman on the porch, gone to the kitchen and returned with a mug of Folgers, offering it to the confused neighbor before closing the door on her.

Now here's the juicy part: Lloyd, against Dianne's family's wishes, had his wife institutionalized. With Lloyd's approval, the shrink put Dianne through a regimen of electroshock therapies more insidious than rehabilitative. By the end of the ordeal, the woman could hardly speak or dress herself. Lloyd divorced her while she was still in the clinic. The broken woman now lives with her sister.

"Well," Kissinger said, putting on a benevolent smile. "You've made the drive out. You might as well stay for dinner."

"I don't know that Gordon *can* stay, honey," Sheila said. "We have a guest we're expecting, remember?"

"What's another seat at the table?"

"It's not a seat. It's food," Sheila said, raising the grocery bags. "I don't think we'll have enough. Anyway, if Gordon wanted to visit, he should have called. A phone call is preferable to a *B and E*."

"I'll make do," I said. "Sheila, you still keep the hearts of baby seals in the freezer, right? For midnight snacks?"

She gave me a look. "No, but there's plenty of rat poison in the garage. Help yourself."

"Who's coming to dinner?"

"Lloyd's agent," Sheila said, her voice nearly quivering with schadenfreudic glee. She knew I'd been struggling to find a sophomore effort, that part of me was terrified of going down in the annals of infant-product history as the man with the talking shitter. I tried to play off her comment. I sat back down and picked through a bowl of pistachios on the coffee table, pulling a few from their shells. "Oh, yeah?" I said. "Time for *Your Baby, Post-Embalmment*, Lloyd?"

"Actually, Gordon, I'm done with the book writing. I've moved on to other projects." Kissinger adjusted his spectacles. "Wait right here," he said. He went to the kitchen and returned with a large glass filled with a liquid so green it looked lab-developed.

"What is it?"

"Try it on for size," he said, handing me the glass.

I gulped it down.

"Well?"

"Interesting," I said. "Full-bodied, with a slight, smoky aroma, a tinge of hawthorn fruit and only the slightest hint of bear piss. Refreshing, Lloyd. What is it?"

Kissinger pulled his hand from behind his back and offered me a bright aluminum can. "I'm calling it Babbleicious for the time being. It's an energy drink for youngsters."

"You mean infants."

"Totally safe. Give it to them forty-five minutes to an hour before naptime. They'll tucker themselves out so thoroughly you'll practically have to defibrillate them back into consciousness."

"Not bad, Lloyd," I said. "You've created the most socially irresponsible product I've heard of in years."

He winked again. "Candy is coming by to go over some prelims on market viability."

"I hate to interrupt shoptalk," Sheila said, "but there's got to be some reason for your visit, Gordon. You are here. I would like for you not to be here. How can we make that come to pass?"

"You have something, something I want."

"You've been saying that for years," Sheila said.

"It's a prototype."

Lloyd perked up. "Oh, yeah?"

"You must've taken the wrong box by accident."

"I don't have any boxes of yours."

"It's okay," I said. "I understand. Things must get blurry when you're leaving your husband. Suddenly. Without reason. To shack up with Professor Pep over here."

"I don't have it, Gordon."

"You have it. It's in the attic or basement."

"If I did have it, which I don't, it'd be in the garage."

"I already checked the garage."

"I'm sorry?" Sheila asked.

"On my way in. I rummaged around a bit."

Sheila ruffled the bags and moved toward the kitchen. "And yet somehow you missed the rat poison," she said. "I don't have time for this. I have a dinner to prepare."

Lloyd and I sat in the living room. On closer inspection, I noticed that in fact he did look younger. There was a glow to his cheeks, a happiness to him I hadn't seen before.

He crossed his legs and leaned in toward me. "How are things? Be honest, Gordon."

"Honestly, Lloyd?" I said.

He nodded.

"I have two pre-pubescent boys staying at my house, ready and willing to commit grand felonies on my order."

Kissinger stared at me for a moment before allowing a grin to fill his face. He chuckled. "Marvelous," he said.

An hour later, Candy Crawford's champagne Mercedes roared up the driveway, headlights strafing the front room windows. Lloyd and I went to the door. Unlike Kissinger's, what I knew of Crawford's personal life was apocryphal. Somebody had once told me that her devotion to the baby business stemmed from her own barren womb, but I didn't believe this. I'd heard the same gossip about nearly every woman in the trade, including Sheila.

We watched Crawford struggle up the steps in green pumps, her hair slumping askance, starboard side. Crawford had all the fashion sense of a stripper trying to mimic a realtor trying to mimic a stripper, but I knew behind the heavy makeup and showy jewelry was an agent so knowledgeable and sly she made my own look like a parochial student. When Lloyd introduced us, Candy made a smile of vague recognition. Then Kissinger brought up Daily Constitutionals. "Oh!" Candy said. "Gordon *Gephardt.*"

Before long, Sheila had dinner ready. What sat before us is difficult to explain. Picture a generous ladleful of creek matter garnished with month-old lawn clippings. A pale lump of yeasty dough sat off to one side. Candy stared despondently over the meal. I held my hands in my lap. But Lloyd relished the paste, pulling spoonfuls of it up to his mouth, some dribbling onto his goatee, his head tilted heavenward, his eyes shut as if in supplication.

A note about my drinking. I am not an anomaly. There is a tremendous amount of libation in this industry. After all, you have chosen to earn a living creating and producing toys for people who have found their lives, within a year or so's time, radically altered, and your product—so they feel—has the power to either transform their child's life for the better or else leave them emotionally crippled and staring at an existence of pathological fucked-upedness.

In the past I'd known Lloyd to be a scotch man, and Sheila had always enjoyed a glass of wine with her meals. And, looking over Candy Crawford, I took her for the kind of woman whose first martini led to a fourth, or shots, or whatever was available. But there was no alcohol in the house, none offered. Whatever buzz I'd worked up with the Riesling was now wearing off. The dinner dragged on hideously.

Finally, at some point, Candy asked Lloyd to show her his new product. She tried it, then put the aluminum can in front of her (using this as a way to push Sheila's meal out of arm's-length). She stared at it for a long while. Then she said, "The can needs alteration. We have to think demographics. Babbleicious isn't something yuppie-type parents are going to trust, not right away."

Lloyd nodded. "Overprotective parents, you're saying."

"I'm saying first-time parents, the kinds of parents who don't want their children napping. The kinds of parents who want to spend every waking hour, even if it means sleep deprivation, with their little bundle. We need to think non-trad. Older types. Parents who've waited to establish their careers."

"Divorcees starting new families," Lloyd added.

"Happy accidents," Candy said. "Fourth children, all the charm worn off, sleep now the most valued commodity within a marriage, sleep bartered for, exchanged with sexual currency."

"Miracle babies," Lloyd said.

Candy nodded. "These are people with income, with demanding jobs and deadlines. They'll find Babbleicious's promise of an hour or two of quiet intriguing. But these are also people who subscribe to advocacy magazines, to the *New England Journal of Medicine*. The types of people who look down on mothers giving their children soda and corn dogs. They want to know a product is not only not unhealthy, but is actually good for their kids."

"Ah, yes," Lloyd said, rubbing his goatee.

"We'll play up the ginseng. The St. John's Wort. Bury the info about triglycerides and Yellow-18. Tell them additional nutritional info can be found on the website, then hide the stuff so deep in HTML code they'll lose interest in trying to track it down."

Sheila turned to me. "Isn't Candy the best?"

"Certainly impressive," I said. Then, "You know, I've been working on a new thing."

"Is that right?" she asked with something less than intrigue, her focus back on the legal pad in which she was furiously scribbling notes.

"It's nothing super, but I think there's a market for it."

"Pitch it to me."

"I'd rather you see it."

She looked up. "You have it? Here?"

"I think so. That is, I think Sheila—before she started banging Lloyd—accidentally stole it."

"Okay, Gordon," Sheila said. She dropped her spoon and crossed her arms.

"Hey," I said, "we can settle this now. Just show me where it is."

"I don't have it."

"Enough," Lloyd said suddenly, putting his napkin in his lap. "Gordon," he said. "How's it sound if after dinner we take a look in the attic? Would that suffice?"

"That would suffice," I told him. "That would suffice sufficiently."

A while passed without conversation. We returned to our meals. Candy was doing a fine job of moving the murky substance around her plate as if through sheer friction the sludge would eventually disappear. I noticed Sheila noticing this. I knew she was doing everything she could to keep quiet, to not raise a stink. Eventually, though, she couldn't help herself.

"Is everything all right, Candy?"

Candy smiled at her. "Oh, certainly. It's just. Well, I hate to ask, dear."

"What is it?"

"Do you have any salt?"

"Salt," Sheila said. She looked at Lloyd.

"I know," Candy said. "I shouldn't ask. I'm a fiend for salt. My doctor has told me to lay off. There's no hope for me."

"Do we have salt, Lloyd?" Sheila asked, not happily.

"I don't think so. Maybe."

"I'll go look," Sheila said.

"I'll help," Lloyd said.

They got up from the table and went into the kitchen.

"So, Candy," I asked after they left. "How on earth did you get into this business?"

"By accident," she said. "I dropped out of Vassar and moved back to Ohio. I had this uncle, you see, a guy I hardly knew who owned a laundromat. He had me working there, managing the books, replacing dryers when they burned out. Do you know what's more predominant in a laundromat than quarters, even dryer sheets? Children. They're everywhere." I gave her an uh-huh. I wasn't listening. What I was doing was watching Lloyd and Sheila. From where I sat I could see them in the kitchen, moving from one cabinet to the next. Sheila opened a top cupboard and went up on her toes to reach for a salt tin, but Lloyd stopped her. He grabbed the Morton's and turned and handed it to her. He said something. They smiled and came out together. I watched Lloyd raise both of his hands slowly and place them on Sheila's stomach. He left them there.

"But I never, ever saw myself doing what I do now," Candy said. "It's strange how life ends up, you know?"

"Sure," I said. "I know."

I've often wondered how the rest of that night might have gone had I not seen Lloyd and Sheila in the kitchen.

After dinner, I let myself out onto the porch. The night held a chill, a burgundy sky wrapping itself around Kissinger's land. I pulled out my cell phone and called home. One of the boys picked up. I could hardly hear his voice over the clamor his friends were making in the background. It was clear they were enjoying themselves.

"Stephen," I said.

"This is Kyle. And who the fuck is this?"

"The man whose house you're in. Listen," I said. "How does midnight sound?"

"What?"

"Midnight," I said. "We still have a deal, right?"

"Oh. Yeah, right. Whatever you want, dude."

Something made of glass shattered, then, and the crowd inside my house cheered. What a strange thing, I thought, to hear joy inside those walls.

"I'm calling, Kyle, to make sure you aren't about to fuck me. We shook hands. I know that means very little to your generation, but—"

"I got it. You'll call again. We'll do whatever you want us to do."

"At midnight."

"Right."

"Good."

I heard something else—something expensive, no doubt—drop to the floor and break. Another cheer. A nail of exhilaration worked itself down the knuckles of my spine. The boys were shirking the governing laws of order, of construction and value and *nice things*, allowing themselves to dance with obliteration.

After the call, I didn't feel much like going back inside. I stayed on the porch, looking out on Kissinger's spread. Beyond the pond the rows of trellises snaked like naked bones into the darkness. Sheila came out onto the porch, pulling a sweater over her shoulders. "Is everything okay, Gordon?" she asked.

"Peachy," I said. "Let me ask you something. What's with the blueberries? I don't get it."

"What do you mean?" Sheila asked.

"Does Lloyd profit from them? Does he sell them?"

"He gives them away."

I chuckled. "Why?" I asked. "He's got to grow them, water them, harvest them—or else pay somebody to do all the work. And you're telling me he doesn't profit, that he gives them away. What's the point? Why do it?"

Sheila came closer to me. "He does it," she said, "because he enjoys doing it."

I looked at her. Perhaps it isn't true that all women look effulgent when they are pregnant, but it was for Sheila. She looked happy, as if now propelled by internal means. She said, "You know, Gordon, I'm glad you came tonight."

I smirked, readied myself for the punch line: *You've reminded me why my divorce attorney was worth every cent*, or, *It's always exciting to witness a car wreck up-close.* Instead she said, "I know you didn't drive out here to pick up a box."

"Oh yeah?" I said, crossing my arms the way I used to when Sheila came home from her therapy sessions. "Enlighten me, then."

Sheila didn't say anything, not right away. When she finally spoke it was in a calm manner. "The other night, Lloyd and I went out to dinner. Somehow we got on the topic of Dianne. You know of Dianne?"

"Sure," I said. "If I remember correctly, she went insane. And Lloyd locked her up."

"He regrets it. Every day, he told me. Not that he left her; he doesn't mean he wishes they were still married. But he regrets the way he treated her toward the end, the way his actions unwound an entire person. He told me he'd like nothing more than to tell Dianne's sister that he isn't the man she knew; he isn't the kind of man who'd do the things he did then. Of course, he can't do that. He can't undo what's been done."

I waited for Sheila to continue. Instead she turned and looked me in the eyes and gave me a weak smile. I knew she was offering me something: the opportunity for both of us to accept defeat, to allow the rage and sadness between us to finally die. She was waiting. All I had to do was say something.

But the heart is easier to barricade than it is to bare. All I had for Sheila was a smirk, a turn back toward the night and Lloyd's spread. "Because he likes it," I said. "How fucking pitiful, Sheila."

Before I left that night, Lloyd took me into his study. He pulled the attic door down and unfolded the ladder. "You'll have to hold this, bud," he told me. "The right leg is missing a washer."

Kissinger made his way up slowly, the top half of him disappearing into the dark attic. He struggled with a string attached to a light bulb; soon, a jaundiced halo came over him. "Gee," he said. "I forgot how much garbage Sheila and I have." He looked down at me and smiled. "Luckily, most of the boxes are marked."

Lloyd sifted through the attic's contents, his bottom half still firmly on the ladder. "Ah," he said after a while. "Think I see something."

I listened to his grunting as he worked a box out of a crevice. My face was hot. I watched his thin haunch dance in front of me. For a moment, I considered letting go of the ladder, allowing it to fold beneath him, or else grabbing his ankles and pulling, his jaw cracking against each rung as he tumbled. Instead, I asked him a question. I asked: "You wouldn't happen to know why Sheila isn't drinking. I mean, there's nothing behind that, is there?"

Kissinger didn't respond immediately. He kept grunting, working the box. "Oh," he said finally, "we've both decided to cut down. Our new meditation instructor requires it as part of the cleansing regimen we're on. The splenic chakra, Gordon, controls kidney function, fatigue, sexual desire. Did you know that?"

"No."

"Did you know, Gordon, that humans are attracted to poison? This is what Dwight, our life coach, tells us, anyway. The things that make us seem happy are also the things that are poisoning our bodies."

"That's fine, Lloyd," I said, "but why don't we cut the maharishi bullshit?"

"There it goes," Kissinger said. He pivoted and stood above me, a dusty, half-caved-in box in his hands. It had my name scribbled on its side. Lloyd came down the ladder and held it out as if it were a present. "Looks like you were right all along, Gordon."

Before I took it, Lloyd looked me in the eye. He didn't wink. He didn't smile. I knew he wasn't going to tell me Sheila was pregnant, even if I asked; that he felt it wasn't my business, that their life together was something that, as soon as this night ended, would no longer contain me—just as Lloyd's no longer contained Dianne—and that together they were moving rapidly toward a place where their pasts could no longer trouble them.

He handed me the box. It was unusually heavy, much heavier than I had anticipated. "I hope what you've been looking for is in there," he said.

Years have passed since that night, but I find myself thinking about it often. Is this what Lloyd meant when he said he wished he could prove he isn't the kind of man who'd done the things he'd done, that he would give nearly anything to prove it?

I wish I could tell you I left Kissinger's on good terms. That I offered my best to Lloyd and Sheila and went back home. That I caught Kyle and Stephen before they did something stupid and told them that they were young and not really arsonists and that love, in whatever granular size Kyle Birchmier was feeling it, can be as difficult as it is beautiful, but you cannot destroy something in order to attain it. I wish I could tell you I've learned this lesson myself.

But that night at Lloyd's, I saw the woman I loved drifting away from a sea of grief while I was left to buoy in its waters. What do you do with something like that? Is there a shore to swim toward, or are there simply depths of the same ugliness, shades of the same kind of drowning?

Kissinger left me alone in his study with the box, presumably so I could check its contents. Instead I put it beneath my arm and walked out into the dining room.

Sheila was sitting near Lloyd. Across from them, Candy Crawford had her pen ready, her eyes on me. She smiled with anticipation. Sheila looked at the box, surprised. Then she looked to Lloyd and back to me. She was ready to say something—they all were—but before she could, I said to her, "Name it Josephine," and left. And I haven't spoken to her since.

—

I called home three times from the road. Nobody answered. At some point a muted moon rose over the highway, sending pale light along the asphalt. I was halfway back when the clock read 12:00.

I'm not sure if I believe it now, but at the time I know what I wanted was to crest the final hill of my neighborhood and see my house—and everything in it—disappearing, turning into raw energy and floating up into the night. I wanted noise and panic. A crowd. I wanted the boys to be there, or maybe hiding in the woods not far away. I wanted them to see what they'd created, to realize the power they had within them, and the power they had over the tangible world.

It would have been simple to begin anew, I thought then, if everything I had was taken from me.

There was no fire. Stepping into the empty house, I saw that the young arsonists and their friends had broken bottles and decanters, china, any number of lamps. They'd taken some of the antlers off the wall in the foyer and, from the looks of it, used them in a game of chicken: gazelle horns broken in two; a moose paddle torn from the bull's taxidermic head. Somebody had used elk tines to tear up a leather sofa in the sitting room—the cushions gutted, exposing puffy innards—and now the rack lay penetrating the arm of the couch, stuck there. Somebody had pissed in the kitchen. Somebody had rolled up a girthy ball of tinfoil and placed it in the microwave.

Later I would find, too, that where Stephen and Kyle had failed to commit the felony I'd hired them to commit, they'd succeeded in petty larceny: the boys had stolen two laptops and a flat-screen television, a DVD player, a stereo system, a few bottles of liquor, a few cigars. The theft did not bother me. I knew I had the boys on surveillance; if I wanted, I could get my things back.

But I wasn't thinking about that, not yet. I went out onto the porch with the box. The four gasoline cans I'd left that morning were still there, near the lounger. Beyond the property a wall of oak, soon to be felled for neighbors' homes, swayed in a chilly breeze. The lake sat perfectly still. I placed the box on top of the lounger. Then I poured gasoline over it, enough to soak the cardboard, to turn it soggy and frail. The house—those rooms—would have to wait; soon I'd be sleeping in one of them. And in the morning, I thought, when light settled back on all of this, I would have to make some decisions, many of which would prove to be difficult. But the first one was easy. I went inside, found a match.

MIRABEAU, THE TRUANT

MIRABEAU COULDN'T SLEEP, so he stole his father's binoculars and went out into the early dawn where, perched in the bed of his father's truck, the boy could see Mrs. Walthrop inside her bedroom, naked. In the daytime he knew Walthrop as the kind old lady who sometimes made him snickerdoodles. But in the drowsy haze of morning, she was a dangerous creature. Her body was a strange topography of mounds and valleys and folds. Mirabeau was eleven years old. The world seemed on the cusp of revealing its secrets.

Mirabeau P. Sloane—the P for Patrick, what his mother called him; Beau to his father; Dicknuts to most of the boys at Duncan Morrow Junior High School, back in Nebraska. He'd been called other things, too. Odd. Slow. A Distraction When He Makes That Horrific Guttural Retching Noise. These were documented and explained to his mother. "Good Lord, Patrick," she'd said to him once after returning from another parent-teacher conference. "Why can't you behave? I raise you so bad you can't but act a fool in public, get me in trouble?"

The truth was Mirabeau had no idea how he'd been acting a fool. There were so many things that didn't make sense to him. Like people. How people went about doing peoplish things.

What he'd learned so far in sixth grade was that among other things people liked to do—talk, eat, laugh—they enjoyed inflicting pain and mortification on one another for no clear reason. Case in point: Grady Mack, a large boy who'd chosen Mirabeau for a de-pantsing last autumn. One moment Mirabeau was standing near his locker with a piece of Laffy Taffy; the next, his penis flopped for all of Morrow Junior High to see. In an attempt to reciprocate the act, to join in on this odd human fellowship of making each other miserable, Mirabeau had put a mechanical pencil through the lining of Grady Mack's stomach.

Now he lived in Texas with his father.

It was 8:05. Soon a school bus would rattle down the street. Mirabeau would watch it go on toward campus, watch its brake lights throb. The boy knew he was meant to be on it. Mirabeau's father was too busy with his own sadness to care. No, it was just Mirabeau and Mrs. Walthrop's white mass, a body promising to make sense of the world.

Mirabeau knew he'd be trudging through snow right now in Nebraska, layers of wool covering him. Here the weather was indecisive. Morning frost melted and gave way to afternoon temperatures that allowed for Mirabeau to go around in an undershirt. He'd spent all of January wandering behind liquor stores and laundromats, finding dead squirrels, beer cans. He went down to a creek that ran along the west side of town—the poor side—and had once spent an entire afternoon tracking a nutria that, when cornered, bit the snot out of his elbow. Mirabeau had had to go to the ER for a rabies shot. He still sported the little moons where the animal's teeth had struck.

But such shiftlessness was old news to him now.

One week ago a space shuttle had fallen from the sky. The debris field was spread over all of East Texas. That morning Mirabeau had been looking in on Mrs. Walthrop. With binoculars trained upward, he saw tracers, debris curlicuing in orange and red flare. Smoke streaked like left-handed pen smudges across the sky. Later there was talk of heavier items raining down: a man two blocks south found runway gear in his aboveground pool. A woman's car windshield had been crushed by a twisted bit of the fuselage. People panicked. They wondered what would fall next. Even Mirabeau's father, who spent most of his time in bed, had moved into the living room to watch the news coverage.

Mirabeau had stood behind the couch, eating a peanut-butter-Vidalia-onion-chocolate-ice-cream-potato-chip-mayonnaise sandwich, his favorite. The bread began to separate; the ice cream was melting. He did his best to hurry—hovering just behind his father, eyes on the television—but a dollop of melted chocolate dropped from the bread onto his father's scalp. The man was too rapt by the disaster footage to do more than run his hand through his hair.

"They dead?" Mirabeau asked.

In response his father looked at him meanly before bursting into tears and locking himself in the bathroom.

"Shit yeah they're dead," Tug Edstrom responded when Mirabeau asked the same question. Tug was two years older and home-schooled, which meant he learned of the suffering of Christ and stole things from Walgreen's. He rode his bicycle listlessly through town. Tug was enormous and the bike was too small for him, but he stayed in perpetual motion, speaking as he cut lazy figure eights in the drugstore parking lot. "Who taught you how to think, the Retard Commission? You reckon if you were in a spaceship and it blew up you'd be able to fly to fucking safety?"

Mirabeau shrugged. He had no answer for either of Tug's questions. It was a sad thing to consider. "They had parachutes," he said, unsure of his own logic.

Tug made another circle around him. He rolled his eyes. "Yeah, and now those parachutes are about this big." He held his index finger and thumb so close together Mirabeau couldn't see any space between them. "Size of your pee-hole. Blammo! All blown the shit up."

The sky had turned an odd, wonderful red, as if it were still ablaze. The town felt empty. In the immediate aftermath of the disaster, people had been told to stay indoors. This was now a hundred-square-mile crime scene; anybody pocketing or hiding debris would be arrested. Black cars and white vans crisscrossed four different counties, racing from one nowhere town to the next. The cars were driven by governmental authorities, Tug told Mirabeau. They interrogated children, poultry farmers, poor folks in trailers.

"But they ain't here over no astronauts," Tug said. "My daddy told me their real reason."

"What is it?"

Tug quit pedaling. He let his bare feet come to rest on the asphalt. He leaned over the handlebars. "To collect my old man's guns." Tug nodded gravely. Mirabeau had been to the Edstrom house only a handful of times. He knew it sat at the end of a gravel road, and that half the roof was corrugated tin; he knew the rooms smelled of burned ketchup and that the walls held dozens of American flags (Tug's brother was in Afghanistan). He also knew that Tug's father spent most of his time outside in what he called The Supply Cabinet. The boys weren't allowed near it, though once, after the man had spent the day drinking Coors and watching the Aggies lose, he'd taken the pair down into the shelter. Inside were hundreds of guns and knives and boxes labeled MRE. Tug's father had taken a rifle off the wall, drew back on the chamber. "This here's a Kalashnikov," he told Mirabeau. "Your daddy have one of these?" The boy shrugged. Tug's father snorted. "Doubtful," he said. "All I've got to say about that is when the Day of Reckoning is at hand, there will be two types of citizens: those who have unfettered access to Kalashnikovs, and those who do not. And who'll have egg on their faces then, I ask."

Tug began pedaling again. He said, "They've been after him for some time. Hell, he doesn't even think there was any spaceship. That's just their cover story; it's their way to have all us God-fearing people looking up at the sky so they can swoop in and take from us what is rightfully ours. Is what my daddy says."

Mirabeau didn't think this was a likely story, but he didn't want to argue. The notion of friendship was new and foreign, and he supposed there was a fine line between having a sleepover and putting a Bic pencil inside somebody's large intestine.

Anyway, he didn't care about the government, or guns, or even space shuttles. What was most pressing was his father, who was looking more and more like an unshaven skeleton.

Mirabeau's father had been a maintenance worker for the small college in town until a professor claimed he'd stolen items from the professor's office. Six astronomy textbooks, which, despite Mirabeau's father's claims of innocence, sat on the coffee table at home. His father had always liked the subject. He liked science fiction movies in which Earthlings traveled vast distances to unoccupied planets and created new civilizations, only to bicker and steal and ultimately learn the real trouble with Earth was the human heart itself.

The night he'd been fired he came home late with alcohol on his breath and told Mirabeau to get in the truck. They'd driven aimlessly through the hills of the piney woods and then out beyond acreage of cut timber—the moon shining on smoking stumps and untenanted backhoes—and eventually up to where the college's observatory and satellite station was located. Mirabeau stayed near the truck while his father tried to jump the fence. It took the man a number of tries. "Are we supposed to be here?" the boy finally asked as his father fell face-first into the dirt on the other side. The man ignored him; he got to his knees and pulled a pair of wire cutters from his jacket and did away with the padlock.

That night, Mirabeau's father fixed a large telescope on the moon and told the boy to look through the viewfinder. He moved it to the bizarre green and yellows of Saturn's rings, to the places where darkness was only interrupted by bright declaratory points of light.

"You see that, Beau?" his father said, gently jostling the telescope into focus. "That's Alpha Centauri, our closest star-neighbor, four-and-a-half light years from Earth. What you're seeing right now," he said, "is light excreted five years ago."

It was all too clear to the boy that his father had been breaking into the observatory for some time, coming out here alone to stare up into the night sky. The thought made the boy sad. There was something in his father's voice that lead Mirabeau to believe that the old man wanted more than anything to be up there, to leave this world and start anew in a place where the people were green, or had extra eyes, or spoke through mucus membranes. Anywhere that would make him feel more at home.

"Isn't it miraculous?" his father asked.

Mirabeau lied and said it was. All he could see were landscapes of cold, dead plains.

Nine days after the shuttle explosion, Mirabeau woke early and snuck into the back room where his father snored like a man hoping for sleep to never end. The boy opened the top drawer of the bureau and pulled the binoculars out of their case and went out to the truck. He peered in on Mrs. Walthrop's room. The woman was there, her body as alien to him as anything happening in the county. All around Mirabeau the forest service was finding smoldering remains, smoky dashes of burnt brush. Governmental authorities parked outside houses and spent hours inside.

Mrs. Walthrop might as well have fallen from the sky. He watched her apply deodorant, slip on a pair of ocher panties. He watched her tuck her breasts inside an old bra that'd been hanging on the doorknob. The school bus came and didn't brake for Mirabeau's home. His attention turned to it; he let his binoculars drop to his chest and gazed at the silhouettes of kids his age behind the dark windows. He understood that these were children he would never know.

Tug rode by that afternoon. He made a sweeping arch in the road before putting down his kickstand.

"I found something," he said. "You gotta see this."

The two times Mirabeau had ridden with Tug he'd had to feel the older boy's sweaty neck and the gelatinous way his flesh moved as he pedaled. It wasn't a pleasant sensation to know firsthand. Still, the look on Tug's face was of high concern.

Mirabeau let himself onto the pegs and draped his arms around Tug's shoulders. They moved down Pecan Street and past the college and across the main road to where the streets were in need of repaving. Tug had strong shoulders. He worked with a grunt. They ditched the bike in the lawn of a house rented by college-looking kids. Mirabeau followed Tug through a pasture, then into the woods, then down a steep hill toward the creek where he'd been bitten by the nutria. Here the February sun, which had coaxed flowers into an early bloom and mosquitoes into a dizzying anger, gave way to the sickly smell of rotten underbrush. Mirabeau forgot about his mother and Nebraska; he forgot about his father. He followed Tug, whose flat feet navigated the steep banks of the creek with a goat's adroitness.

In the stagnant water lay a torn-wide canister. Around it, circular orbs gleamed like pearls with diameters larger than silver dollars.

"What are they?" Mirabeau asked.

"What are *you*, the world's dumbest dumbass?" Tug said, wiping sweat from the light hair growing on his lip. "They're Petri dishes."

Mirabeau picked one up. It held a clear liquid.

"Big deal," he said.

"Big deal?" Tug dropped three of them into a purse he'd made out of the bottom of his shirt. "These things come falling out of space filled with alien goop. They're worth about a million bucks apiece, is what big deal."

Mirabeau examined the one in his hands. The dish looked half-filled with piss. Nothing swam in its liquid, so far as he could tell. He shook it to make sure.

"You can have them," he said, and dropped the dish back into the mud.

Tug rushed to pick it up. He gave Mirabeau a wild-eyed look. "Sheeit. I can't take them all with me. That's how you get caught. We've got to divide them up, hide them, wait for things to settle. Then we'll sell them on eBay and retire to the Kasbah." Tug held three of them out for Mirabeau, who looked them over again before putting them in his pockets.

—

At home, his father was awake. Mirabeau spotted his hairy shoulders pacing the kitchen. He had the phone to his ear.

"No, Regina. I'm not belittling your beautician career. I know you...that's what I'm saying...no...no... No, Charlie doesn't have anything to do with this... Yes... That's right... You've told me Charlie is twice the man I... He can't stay here... I know he's my son, Regina; I was there during conception if you're... Of course he's going to school. What kind of a fath... Because, he can't. He can't stay here. I don't think it's a good envir... Because...no...don't bring Charlie into this. I don't want to talk to Char... Yes, Charlie? Hi. Listen. I need to speak to Regina; it's a private mat... It's about Beau, yes. Well, no. That's the...as I was telling Regina, I don't think this is the right...what I'm trying...what I'm try...what I'm trying to say is that he needs to move back to Nebraska."

Mirabeau slipped past the kitchen and into his father's bedroom. He opened the second drawer—the junk drawer, where the old man kept pocketknives and coins flattened by trains and a little pamphlet titled *We Are Not Alone*. The boy pulled the Petri dishes from his pockets and slipped them beneath the layer of junk. On the ride back from the creek, he'd decided to keep them, to give them to his father. To hell with Tug and eBay. The Kasbah sounded cruddy. They were a gift now. Summer would come. The governmental agents would disappear. Years would pass—who knew?—and then one day his dad would find them and know that they were from his son. And he would finally have his own piece of the universe. It would make him happy.

Mirabeau could hear his voice from the kitchen.

"Can you put Regina back on? She's on? Right now? I'm speaking to both of you, is that... I see. Yes, Regina, that's what I'm trying to explain. I don't feel I can provide the kind home that... No...of course he's in school... Yes, he has friends. I don't know their names. Some fat kid on a bike. I'm not in the right headspace to take care of... Headspace. Headspace, Charlie. Yes, it's a word. I'm not in the right... There are plenty of words you don't know, Charlie, you dolt. Listen to me. Will you... I'm saying... What? What? I know he's your husband,

Regina. I was your husband, too, once, or don't you... I can call him whatever I wa...his feelings? His feelings! Okay, you're right. Charlie, I'm sorry I called you a dolt. Can we move on? As I was saying, I can't do it. I simply cannot. I'm in a strange... Are you crying, Charlie? I said I was...that's right: I'm not in a very good place right now, headspace-wise. That's all there is to it. Mirabeau doesn't... I'm saying he can't... You have to come pick him up, Regina. Hello? Regina? Hello?"

It is the fantasy of every eleven-year-old to never go to school. Inside the bright and sterile confines of their classrooms, they feel certain they're missing out on life and its pleasures, which are being doled out in unjust portions to their parents, who don't know how blessed they are, who use their time paying bills and running to the dry cleaners. Beyond the mundane walls of the school, time is slipping by while people ignore the chance for the miraculous.

Mirabeau felt this way at Duncan Morrow. But now that he was living on the other side of the fantasy—now that he was free to roam as he pleased—he felt otherwise. He missed school. It was a sentiment he would never share with another living creature for fear that its utterance would somehow instantly undo his freedom. As soon as he said the word *miss* and *school*, he would suddenly be inside one, at a desk, the teacher asking him for the angles to an isosceles triangle. But the missing remained.

At eleven years old, with the firsts of hormonal changes beginning, Mirabeau was also learning what true loneliness felt like.

He guessed this new loneliness had something to do with how fast everything moved. It was March, suddenly. Save for a short sound bite on the news, people had begun to forget about the space shuttle. Temperatures rose. The man with the aboveground pool moved to Florida. Tug Edstrom's father shot himself in the foot.

The shot was non-fatal but required the amputation of two toes. There was going to be an investigation into The Supply Cabinet and its contents. For three nights, Tug had had to stay with Mirabeau and his father. It was Mirabeau's first time to host a sleepover.

As it turned out, sleepovers weren't as fun as he'd always assumed them to be. For one, your new bedmate could snore like a full-grown man who'd swallowed a buzz saw. And Mirabeau's father explained to the boy that, as a guest, Tug was in command of activities. If Mirabeau wanted to climb a tree but Tug wanted to play *Red Dead Redemption* for twelve straight hours, the Xbox won out.

There were some positives. Mirabeau's father began to shower and dress in slacks. He tried to appear normal. He cooked the boys Hamburger Helper, watched television with them. During the day, when Tug's mother arrived for school lessons (she always appeared in nice clothes, with her hair coiffed, though her eyes were puffy and gave away the shock and anxiety of her husband's possible pending jail time), Mirabeau's father acted as though Mirabeau, too, were home-schooled. He thanked her for letting the boy sit in on their lessons, and offered to pay her for her time.

On the third night, Tug turned Mirabeau's small TV to a scrambled cable channel and slapped its side, hoping to clear the picture.

"Think I can make out a tit," he said.

"Where?"

"Between the blue and orange waves."

"That's no tit."

"You wouldn't know a tit from a watermelon," Tug said. He slapped the television a few more times but gave up when it went to static. He sighed. He looked around Mirabeau's bedroom. "Jesus, this place is boring. Don't you have a computer or something? Some place where I can see a tit?"

"Dad has one," Mirabeau said. He was trying to make a noose out of his old tae kwon do belt. "It's in his bedroom, but there's no Internet. It's got Minesweeper."

Tug looked at him. "For fuck's sake. Minesweeper? I'd rather play with my toes." They were quiet for a while. Then Tug's face brightened. "Just thought of something," he said. "The dishes."

Mirabeau shrugged, though he knew what Tug meant.

"The fucking Petri dishes." Tug stood up. He was excited, flushed.

Mirabeau tightened the knot on his makeshift noose and thought about how if he'd taken tae kwon do seriously he would've been able to diffuse this situation with a simple roundhouse-kick. "I've done away with them," he muttered.

Tug's face dropped. "What's that mean?"

"It means you can't have them. They're gone. You might as well forget—" The wind came out of his lungs before he could finish. Tug had Mirabeau on the floor. The boy's shoulders were pinned down by Edstrom's giant knees.

"You gaywad," Tug said. "You dumb retard. Those were my meal tickets! Those were my way out of here!" He had his fingers in Mirabeau's mouth, his nostrils. He was doing serious business, and though Mirabeau couldn't be certain, it sounded as if he were about to cry. "You shithead," Tug said. "You fuck everything up. Everything."

Mirabeau was able to get Tug's hands away from his face. "You ain't getting them," he coughed. "You ain't. You ain't."

"Then I'll have to kill you, Dicknuts."

Tug's weight came down on Mirabeau like a tidal wave. He had his large hands around the boy's throat. Mirabeau felt blackness coming on. He forced Tug's paw away from his neck long enough to let out a gurgled, shrill cry: "I got tits!"

Tug paused.

"I can show you tits," Mirabeau gasped.

"I don't want to see yours."

"I mean real ones," Mirabeau said. Tug's weight lessened, though he kept his knees on Mirabeau's shoulders. The circulation in Mirabeau's hands had been cut off; he couldn't feel his fingers. "Real live ones," he said.

Tug collapsed on the floor next to him. Mirabeau sat up and shook his hands and reached for his throat. Tug was staring at him, eyeing his move. "Bullshit," the boy said.

"I'll trade you," Mirabeau said. He considered what he was saying. Mrs. Walthrop had been his own discovery, and while most mornings left him more confused than ever, he still held hope that his view through the binoculars would lead him to understanding what it was that confused him. On the other hand, he wanted the Petri dishes for his father, who, despite the showers and clean shirts and dinners, still had a distraught look in his eyes. "We'll trade," he said again.

Tug agreed. He asked Mirabeau to show him what he promised. Mirabeau explained that they'd have to stay up all night. Tug looked skeptical—for a moment Mirabeau braced himself for another attack—but finally nodded.

The boys stayed up. They drank soda. They played video games. They put an old ventriloquist doll Mirabeau had been given for his seventh birthday on trial, found him guilty, then hanged him from the bedpost using the noose Mirabeau had fashioned. They drank RC Cola and ate pizza. They found some old GI Joes in the closet and melted their legs with a cigarette lighter Tug had stolen from Walgreen's. "Ahhhhhh!" the GI Joes screamed, their feet curling and letting off putrid black smoke. They watched a movie, then another. The night turned gray. Mirabeau worried that if Mrs. Walthrop wasn't there in the morning, he would lose his friend. Tug's eyes began to close. Mirabeau nudged him, told him to stay awake. When the time was right, Mirabeau snuck into his father's room and stole the binoculars.

They went out into the morning. Mirabeau helped Tug into the back of the truck.

"All right," Tug said. "Time to pay up."

Mirabeau fixed the binoculars on the bedroom window next door. He adjusted the view, waited. The room was empty, dark. Tug sighed. Then she appeared, fresh from the shower, a towel around her waist. "There," Mirabeau said. "She's there."

Tug snatched the binoculars from him. Mirabeau guided his aim. Tug looked on for a while. His mouth dropped open. Mirabeau asked for the binoculars. Tug shrugged him away with an elbow.

"Miraculous," Tug whispered.

Mirabeau had assumed the crunching of leaves nearby was the sound of a cat at play or a dog circling a place to do its business, and so it was too late to react when a man appeared in his periphery. He came from around the back of the Walthrops' house, in between the two properties, wearing a floppy hat and carrying a rake. Mirabeau felt the blood drain from his cheeks.

"Boys?" the man said. "Boys."

Tug dropped the binoculars. They smashed against the bed of the truck with a loud crack. Then Tug tried to flee, but his foot caught the tailgate, and he toppled over the rear bumper and onto the driveway. He stood, knees bloodied, his right palm scraped white. He looked at Mirabeau, then at Mr. Walthrop, before loafing across the lawn toward his bicycle. He was gone before Mirabeau could move.

Walthrop looked confused. He came toward Mirabeau, stopped short, peeked into his own bedroom window. His face appeared unable to form itself into one particular expression. He was confused at what he saw, then recognizant, then alarmed.

His face changed again. "My wife," he said, looking up at Mirabeau. "I've known her since she was a girl. We won't be together much longer." He looked back at the window. Mirabeau wanted nothing more than to leave, to get away. It wouldn't be the last time he'd feel this way. In some months, when Charlie comes to pick him up and drive him back to Nebraska. Or at the beginning of the next school year, when the boy will expect his reputation as Dicknuts to precede him, only to find nobody remembers the de-pantsing or the Bic pencil incident or that Mirabeau ever went to school with them at all. And there will be the years his father's sadness will be a thing culled only from memory—a new wife, a baby daughter—and, oddly, feel to Patrick nostalgic and cloying in an inaccurate but indulgent way. His father's new wife will require a new house, and most of the furniture Patrick remembered would disappear in a garage sale, including the Petri dishes—*10 cents each.* There will be Patrick's own wife and family, his own battle with depression, his own troubles. He'll be unable to recall what he knew just then, which was that nobody felt at home in the world. Everybody was filled with desire and longing. His father wanted to move to a different planet. Tug's own was waiting for the end times. The space shuttle explosion had injected the town with a cause to feel alive and terrified and filmed and important. But it hadn't lead to anything new. It hadn't shifted anybody's life in a way that would last. It was already a footnote in history.

Mr. Walthrop smiled at the boy. "Can I see your binoculars?" he asked.

A WORLD IN WHICH NONE OF THIS SHIT MATTERS

THE BUS ROLLS ACROSS THE BARE SOUTH TEXAS FLATS, windows down and dust stinging Daniel's scalp. November, and the air still hot—the air always hot here—and the kids, some forty of them, a choral of piercing shrieks and bat-like ringing and glee glee glee; and though Daniel has never liked any of this (the children; the bus and looming lighthouse; how the dry air cracks membranes in his nose and forces him to shove wads of toilet paper inside to stop the bleeding), he smiles.

He won't not smile; not today.

Daniel is leaving his live-in girlfriend, Annie, just as soon as this last chore is done. And no, he won't do the noble thing and wait until after the holidays. He will not work through this rough patch, and he damn sure isn't going back to couple's counseling. This time he's quitting her for good. Daniel can have his stuff packed and in his Subaru within half an hour. What's there to take, anyway? A few ties and pairs of slacks, a can of mink oil, *The Book of Mormon* from that year he let a handsome kid in the doorway convert him. He's tried once before, got as far as Dairy Queen before capitulating to that sudden rush of fear— the fear of not knowing where he was headed or what he'd do once he got there. Now he knows. He's going to wrap himself in the polite shawl of Topeka, Kansas, a place he's never been but has always liked the sound it makes. *Toe–pee–kuh.* 1,039 miles due north.

Todd sits three seats ahead of Daniel, pulling off another boy's hat and throwing it into the aisle, laughing maniacally, watching the kid squirm to retrieve it. Annie's got a badger on her hands, a real nasty kid. Daniel is not Todd's father. He's done his best. The kid is a genetic terror. It's in his blood to destroy, hurt, chicane, tease, tailgate, maim, deflower, skulk, misdemean, knock, spoil. Daniel's no psychic. He's seen all of this already, in Todd's father.

The bus jerks across a narrow causeway and onto the island—a sandbar, really—and through Port Elizabeth. Nothing much of a town. Its 3,000 citizens are listless and sunstroked, rich from offshore oil. The class moves toward the edge of the city, the edge of the state, the final tip of this country, where, on a knoll of beach grass and against an unseasonably bright sky, a lighthouse sticks out like a long, smooth bone.

They've been coming here since Daniel was in school, a sloppy tie-in to the section on Aquatic Science. Really, it is a way for the ISD to pencil a cheap field trip into the curriculum. A half-dollar a head in his day. Five bucks now.

The driver farts the airbrakes. Mrs. Sadler, Todd's fifth-grade teacher, stands up and tries to instruct the students. But the kids are already swarming the aisle. When Daniel tries to get up, he's shoved back into his seat by the wave. This is going to be a long day, he thinks. He's glad he brought a joint.

Daniel agreed to chaperone months ago, forgot about it until, Saturday night, Annie reminded him. They were fighting again. Listerine again. Listerine was the reason for most of their arguments. He keeps a mini bottle of the antiseptic in his sports coat and sucks on it every chance he gets, intervals usually of forty-five minutes. She's never understood this. Some people like cigarettes and take smoke breaks, he once tried to explain. She stared at him.

So often the cap comes loose and green liquid soaks into the fabric of his pockets. It'd happened that afternoon. Annie stood over the coat, scrubbing at the stain. "A closet of ruined jackets," she said, "and for what? I bought this one for you, for Valentine's. I saved for it, ordered it from the Dillard's catalog. I went all out, Daniel. And now look."

"I'll take it to the cleaners Monday," he said. He sat at the kitchen table, thumbing through a magazine.

"What will you wear to the lighthouse? You need to dress decently. You'll be representing Todd and me."

"The lighthouse?" Daniel said. He'd blocked the place out of his mind.

"It won't come out," Annie said, her hand and sponge lost in foamy stain remover. "You've really fucked this one up. I have to hand it to you, Dan. When you put your mind to it, you can really move mountains."

Near the base of the knoll, with the lighthouse towering over them, Mrs. Sadler shouts, "Can you *please* gather the Blue Team, Mr. Albright? And put your armband on."

Daniel pulls the blue armband from his stained pocket and rolls it over his bicep. He mumbles, "Blue Team. Over here."

"You're the captain, Mr. Albright," Mrs. Sadler says. "Act like it!"

"Jesus," Daniel says. He watches the fifth-graders chase one another around the bus, watches Todd hip toss that same, poor boy into the dirt. Daniel screams, "Blue Team! For Chrissake's, Blue Team!"

The tour guide is a rail-thin girl with a voice like a finch. She speaks to the children with exaggerated hand gestures, trying to keep their attention. As she makes important points on nautical mile conversion and the way lighthouses work, Daniel keeps his eyes on Todd. Annie hasn't taken him to the barber in over a month and his sandy brown hair hangs past the collar of his polo shirt. From profile, Daniel can also make out a near-white fuzz running from the boy's sideburn down his cheek, whirring near his jaw line. Daniel's never noticed this before.

Each year, the Annie in him disappears, and Todd takes on more of his father's traits.

It's not just the Listerine.

They grew up together in the same small town: Daniel, Annie, and Todd's father, Leland. Annie and Leland were two years older, popular kids always seen in a blur, racing off to a kegger or tearing down the highway in Leland's hatchback, their bodies filled with rye and Quaaludes. Their relationship was one of those tragic love tales, the foibles and fallouts known to everyone walking the halls of Charles Goodnight High. The time Leland, drunk, crushed Annie's daddy's trashcan with his car and was barred from ever stepping foot in Annie's house again. The time he beat the shit out of her for flirting with a buzzcut from Fort Hood. The marriage proposals; the plans to elope; plans stymied; plans reneged. The breakups; tears tears tears; suicide threats; tender moments outside the junior prom; the makeups; tears tears tears; oral carnality in the backseat, on back roads, at the beach.

Daniel lived alone with his grandmother. Not poor but a girl of the Depression, she saved everything. She jarred fruits and froze casseroles, had a row of drying Ziploc bags hanging constantly from the kitchen towel rack.

Daniel had no money for a car when he turned sixteen. When he asked the old woman for a loan, she said, "You got plenty a time to drive, boy. Right now, there's a perfectly good tandem Schwinn just sitting there in the carport."

Daniel was the only sophomore without a license. He had to trek four and a half miles from his grandmother's house to the high school. The rusted rear wheel bleated out over the thin roads around town. You could hear it rising above the plain, first taking it for the strange song of a dying bird, but soon enough seeing the fat, sweaty boy crossing the road on an absurdly long bike, the back seat empty.

Once, during Spanish class, someone blurted out that Danny Albright looked like a Mr. Potato Head toy. The nickname stuck. Older boys learned his route, crept behind him and stood in the backs of pickups, screaming: "Hey, you lost Mrs. Potato Head! She fell off the back of your bike. Keep at it, Mr. PH! You're almost home! Boy, here you go! Look at you now, the last of the bicyclists!"

There was Annie in all of this, any number of boys orbiting her like satellite moons. The general consensus was that she resembled Joan Baez. She had a certain rugged and raw beauty. There was Caddo blood in her. These boys who followed her kept their distance, knowing she was with Leland and that Leland—sixteen, already a full mustache, a face that'd been eternally skewed to look as if he wouldn't think twice before beating you to death with a lawn sprinkler—was someone worth avoiding.

Annie didn't know Daniel, not until a decade after he graduated college and moved back to Texas to take care of his emphysemic grandmother and walked into a bar near the county line and found her alone at a table in the corner, her looks nearly gone. She sat tiny in her chair with her arms crossed, drunk.

He sat at the bar and ordered a drink, turning so often to glance at her. Annie put her giant handbag on the table and dug through it, came out empty-handed, scanned the room. Her gaze landed on him. She waved him over. At first Daniel turned back to the bar, sat slouched over his pilsner. She was still waving when he glanced again.

He walked to her table. She said, "Look, man," and pointed at her purse, "so I have three bucks on me and I was sitting here counting my cigarettes and, well, there's only two left, two and a half if you count the one I partly smoked after work. And I was thinking, well I can either spend these three dollars on another drink, but then I don't have any money for cigarettes. And cigarettes always come first." She laughed. "So I'm wondering if maybe there's one kind soul left in this town willing to buy a girl another brew."

He smiled. "Sure," he said and went to the bar and ordered and came back and sat down across from her. She thanked him and lit the half-smoked cigarette and blew out a thick cloud, took a drink and sighed and slouched in her chair. They didn't speak for a while. She looked around him but not at him, not for a time. Once she did she grinned and nodded at the drink, but remained quiet.

Daniel said, "You're Annie Gomez."

"Do you know me from somewhere?"

"We went to high school together. Charles Goodnight. I'm Daniel Albright."

"Oh, right." She nodded. "Daniel Albright." He watched her try to place him. "How've you been?"

"Great," he said. "Just got out of college."

"College," she said.

He smiled.

"What are you doing back here?"

"My grandmother. I'm taking care of her, you know, until—"

"Oh." Annie slapped her palm against the table. She laughed loud enough to draw looks from the few roughnecks huddled at a pool table. "Riiiight. *That* Daniel. The guy on the bicycle."

He didn't say anything. He kept his smile intact.

"The tandem bike guy."

"That was a long time ago," he said. "But, yes, that's me." He waited. He thought about the Schwinn for a moment, blue as a robin's egg except where corroding, the pearlescent vinyl seats torn and shredded, foam-guts leaking out. Daniel thought he was the only one who remembered. He didn't expect Annie to bring it up.

Then he asked her a question he already knew the answer to. "How's Leland? That's his name? Leland?"

Her smile faded. She stubbed her cigarette in the ashtray. "I was stupid enough to think he was going through a phase." She said, "I had his kid, you know. A boy. I named him Todd. That was Leland's middle name."

They had a few more drinks, stayed until the bar closed. She tottered outside with his help, and they leaned against her green Chevette. He found the keys in her purse and opened the door. She put her hands on his shoulders and whispered, "I always wanted to fuck on a tandem bike."

He drove her to her house.

He moved in after his grandmother died that spring.

He's never forgotten that she hadn't forgotten the bike.

—

Aside from the lighthouse, there is a gift shop and a cafeteria and a tour of the Sears Roebuck house that served as keeper's quarters. The students are filed past every historical marker. They pause while the young tour guide reads aloud. Each time, though, before she's anywhere near finished, the kids are throwing rocks and laughing. Teachers' pets shush the others, but no one pays attention to them, not even Mrs. Sadler.

"This was where the Palmer family lived while Mr. Thaddeus Palmer worked as the keeper," the tour guide says. The class shuffles into the musty living room. "Can you imagine, at one time, there were eleven people living in here?"

"No," the class says. Daniel has to admit that it's pretty unbelievable. There are only two bedrooms, a kitchen, and the small living space where they are standing. He looks over at Todd. He imagines the three of them living in this musky house. Would their lives be any different? Would their lives be better?

The day is getting hotter. They pass beneath the tower and the tour guide says, "This particular lighthouse has withstood three different hurricanes. It is the only working lighthouse in Texas open to the public. After lunch, we'll go up to the lantern room. From there we'll be able to see Texas, the Gulf, and even part of Mexico. All at once!"

Hours before the wreck that killed Leland, Daniel biked to the grocery store with a list from his grandmother. He rode slowly from their neighborhood down McKinney Avenue and past the high school, through the pink-gray last light of evening and under the orange blaze of the store's wide sign. He checked out and hung the overstocked plastic bags from the bike's handlebars.

Tired, he stopped for a break in the high school parking lot. The night was muggy and sweat darkened a V into the top of his shirt. He folded out the kickstand near some hedges and wandered knee-deep into the shrubbery and unzipped his shorts and started to pee. He looked down onto the twinkling lights along Lamar Street. It was quiet except for an occasional breeze. Someone nearby was burning trash; he smelled charred plastic.

The squeal of tires and a roaring engine came from behind. Daniel turned, penis still hanging from his shorts, and saw Leland's hatchback cut across the parking lot. The car stopped near the gym. Leland hopped from the driver's-side window. What Daniel didn't see—not until Leland was already on top of the stranger, hitting him, holding him by the collar and jabbing him in the nose, the side of the face, the back of the skull—was the slim silhouette of another boy who'd been moving along the darkened sidewalk encircling the school.

Daniel squatted in the bushes. His right hand shook and his kidneys throbbed, something that happened any time he received a jolt of adrenaline. Leland stood over the stranger, shouted, "Don't ever come near my girl again. Don't ever touch her, you bitch."

The kid stuttered and said in a shrill whine, "I don't know what you're talking about, man."

"Fuck you," Leland said and clenched his fists and drew back as if to hit him again. But he didn't. He stood like that with his back to Daniel, straddling his victim. "You think I'm stupid? You think I don't know what's going on? Fuck you, bro. Fuck you." He said it again. "Fuck you, dude." Then he slapped the guy in the face, lightly. Leland cackled, popped him again, playfully. "Huh?" he said, over and over. "Huh? Huh? Huh?" slapping the boy, the boy lifting his hands as if in prayer and Leland batting them away. "Huh? Huh?" the sound of his voice like a chugging, struggling engine. "Huh? Huh? Huh?"

Finally two of Leland's friends fell out of the hatchback and came to him. They said, "Okay, Lee, he's had enough." They grabbed his shoulders, but Leland pulled away. He slapped the kid three more times before walking to the car, spitting, wiping his lips.

He and the others lit cigarettes. They stood for only a second in heavy sighs before piling into the car. Daniel watched the pup tents bob on the roof as the hatchback tore across the asphalt.

The beaten stranger had gotten to his knees but no further. The kid held his nose with his hand. Daniel sunk lower into the bush. He waited. He heard an odd moaning noise and looked over and watched in horror as the tandem Schwinn tilted from its kickstand and crashed against the pavement. Cans of asparagus and corn rolled down the hill. A carton of half-and-half leaked onto the cement. The stranger glared across the parking lot to where Daniel felt his head budding from the hedge like a swollen berry. Neither of them moved. Daniel sensed the stranger required something from him. He stood up. He felt the warm wind against the tip of his penis, against the dime-sized spot he'd made on the front of his shorts.

He opened his mouth as if to say something, but the stranger had gotten to his feet now and wiped the blood from his face against the sleeve of his jacket, staring at Daniel. Daniel was quiet. He rustled out of the shrubbery and picked up the bicycle and, before long, had the groceries back in their bags. He climbed onto the banana seat and left.

—

As soon as the children are corralled for lunch, Daniel sneaks behind the cafeteria and lights the joint. It's nothing good—some cut-rate weed he bought from a teenager down the block. Not far from the dining room he finds a burial ground and walks toward the historical marker. His eyesight is cloudy and he feels jittery and giggly, but concentrates on the words:

PALMER FAMILY CEMETERY

Est. 1926

Here lie all members of the Thaddeus Palmer family, including two wives, Ellen and Rose, and nine sons. Absent from this gravesite are three of Palmer's daughters, whose bodies were lost to the sea.

Lost to the sea. Daniel wonders why anyone would want this kind of life. Manning a light for people you'll never see, taking responsibility for lives you'll never know.

"What are you doing?"

The voice comes from behind him, cutting through the silence. Daniel spins around, hides the joint behind his back. He coughs out a curl of smoke. Todd stands twenty or thirty yards away, holding half a sandwich.

"I needed some fresh air," Daniel says. He drops the joint and steps backward, putting a heel over it. "That cafeteria was giving me indigestion, all the noise."

"Mom says you shouldn't smoke."

"I'm not smoking."

"I saw you, Daniel."

"Yeah, well. I've asked you not to call me that."

Todd moves closer. The kid takes a giant bite out of the sandwich and cocks his head and frowns, as if he's really thinking over what Daniel has just said. "Mom said it's all right to call you Daniel."

Daniel sighs. He turns back to the cemetery, pulls out his mini-bottle of antiseptic and downs what's left.

"Why do you drink so much mouthwash?" Todd asks.

Daniel looks at him. He counts twenty more seconds, spits, runs his jacket sleeve across his mouth. "I don't drink it."

"You carry it everywhere, I know that," Todd says. "It stains your clothes. Your lips look green all the time. Mom says it's OCD, that you have a problem. She says you're nervous. But she used a different word."

"Neurotic," Daniel says.

"Yeah," Todd says. "That's it. She says you use Listerine as a crutch. She says it's got something to do with your childhood. That you have an oral pixilation."

"You're mom can't find her ass with both hands," Daniel mumbles.

"What?"

The wind changes and picks up and carries the stench of rotting fish, rustles the chain-link fence around the gravesite. "All I said is that Annie isn't a dentist. If she were she'd tell you, Todd, that there's not a trace of gingivitis anywhere in my mouth; there's not a speck of plaque and no sign, *no sign*, of gum disease."

Todd walks closer. He comes within feet of Daniel. The boy crosses his arms, squints. His cute cheeks are gone and his head now resembles an arrowhead. His eyes, too. They seem permanently dilated. Daniel's certain this is Leland's DNA coming through, coming late, blitzing Annie's contribution—relegating her genes to the minor traits, the circular ears and thin top lip. Leland's soul is in him, Daniel thinks, stoned and jittery.

"Are you enjoying the field trip?" he asks.

"It sucks." Todd eyes him, looking for something. Daniel doesn't know what to do. The kid makes him nervous, his glare sharp and probing.

"All right, Todd," Daniel says, sighs. "I'm going to tell you something. I want you to listen. It's important, you understand? Here it is: take care of your mother. Don't act up. Know that I tried. But some people won't take it, even if you offer it every day; they don't want your help. You can tell a woman you're different and she's different, and that people grow up and move on and become different people— certainly they become different people than they were in high school. They shouldn't be pigeonholed by shit that happened fourteen years ago. I tried with you, too, Todd. I bought a football for your birthday. You deflated it and wore it as a hat, strutted around the living room proud at what you'd done to my gift.

"Do you remember that time I came outside to weed-eat the lawn and saw you picking on that redheaded boy from across the street? James, I think was his name. Or Jimmy. Anyway, you had Jimmy in a headlock. You were giving him a noogie. You moved on to Indian rug burns. I went inside and told Annie. I told her what I'd seen, how you were acting, how that kid's face had turned as red as a tomato—as red as his hair. And do you know what your mother said to me? Do you?"

Todd's pointed little face doesn't change, not for a second.

"She told me to ignore it. She said, 'This is just how healthy boys act.'" Daniel scoffs, throws his hands into the air. "Healthy. What am I supposed to do with that, Todd? Well? You can't fight dim with dim, Todd. Remember I told you that."

The boy doesn't respond. A bell goes off in the cafeteria, followed immediately by the clamor of children and the rush of bodies. Daniel, his vision still hazy and slow, locks eyes with the boy, waits for him to say something. There's an instant when Daniel thinks he's gotten through and he and Todd have connected on a serious level and, after this—maybe months or years or even a decade after this—Todd will look back on the moment, the sermon, and use it to better himself.

But Todd rolls his eyes. "Whatever." He adds, in a low voice, "Mr. Potato Head."

Daniel's face warms. His throat parches. "What'd you just say?"

"I said, 'Fuck you, Dan.' You're weak, dude. I've known it for as long as I can remember."

The boy moves in a strange way, with a jerk and a roll of his shoulders, as if he's about to lunge at Daniel. But Todd only looks him up and down and turns and trots to where, on the far side of the lunchroom, the students are amassing—the tops of their heads bobbing in a large circle. Daniel stays, his mouth open, stunned. He's never heard Todd say anything like this. He scratches his scalp again. He faces the cemetery and pulls out the bottle of Listerine. He tilts it upward, sucking the last few drops, and stares at Palmer's headstone. "Some fucking way to make a living," he says.

—

The young historian is replaced by a fat man wearing a wide-brimmed straw hat. He guides the class to the top of the lighthouse. As the children climb the steps, the stairwell fills with the stench of post-lunch gas: Coca Colas and Doritos; bologna and Swiss and pepperoni Lunchables. He sticks to the back of the procession, taking his time. In what little light the stairwell offers, Daniel watches the new guide's hatband shimmer like the scales of a trout. It reminds him of the hat Annie wore when she gardened. He used to help her, just after he'd moved in—when Todd was an infant. He'd mow and weed-eat, and, upon taking a break, watch Annie hunched over in the sod planting daisies and petunias. On those nights, on the nights when it was just the two of them—Todd already asleep—they'd cover themselves in a tangle of quilts and pillows and burrow into an overstuffed chair and do nothing but watch and listen to the savage wind shove at their windowpanes and whip through the trees. A small lamp turned on behind them, shadows on the parquet floor, the sensation they'd almost gotten away with something. They'd almost reached the point of outrunning their pasts.

This was not enough. He couldn't stick around for memories and near-misses.

Todd has never called him Mr. Potato Head before.

The new guide says, "You can see the entire island of Port Elizabeth from up here. And out there, well, that's the Gulf of Mexico. To your left, yes, that's Matamoros, you're right about that. And if you follow me, we can look out onto the great state of Texas—just over that bridge."

The kids scream with delight. They point and shout, "I can see where I live! I can see where I live!" though they've mistaken houses lining the shoreline for their own town, Daniel's town, sitting some thirty-plus miles to the north. He wishes they could see where they're from, though, and gaze onto the soot-colored roofs of their neighborhood from a different point of view and know that what's familiar can sometimes look alien and bizarre. Mostly though, Daniel wishes the lighthouse were taller, as tall as the Tower of Babel or the lost beacon of Alexandria. He wants to stand in the lantern room of a building so towering that it's impossible to see the ground. From such a height, he could gape at the highway cutting through the center of the state, follow that road with his eyes, watch it grow faint, ogle the place where it ends, *Toe–pee–kuh*, and all the obscene joy as thick as fog, people of the plains walking the streets with faces stretched into exclamation: *I am fulfilled! I have been rewarded! I don't dread!*

They file onto the bus and Daniel takes a seat to himself, slouches, sighs. He struggles to make eye contact with Todd. There's more that needs to be said. But Todd is forcing a kid to hit himself with his own balled fist. Was Leland like this? When, fifteen or sixteen years ago, fifth-grade Leland was shuttled out here on the same field trip to the same island, did he abuse and batter his classmates? Or maybe this thing with Todd is something else. Maybe Leland was a swell child—a sandy-haired boy with a dimpled grin and kindness sweating from his pores. And only later something in him shifted.

It doesn't matter. When he hits Topeka, the first thing Daniel will do is disremember Leland and Todd and Annie. He'll disremember the night in the gym parking lot. The night he met Annie. Today. It will be a new world, a world in which none of this shit matters, and there's nothing that seems so sweet to him now.

The driver presses on the accelerator. They flatten out onto the mainland. Soon they pass the county line and before long they'll be downtown. When they get to Annie's house, Todd will immediately dash into the back bedroom to watch cartoons. Daniel will give him an ice cream sandwich, maybe two, maybe three if that's what it takes to distract him.

Daniel can have his things packed and in his Subaru in half an hour, maybe less. There's so much of it he can leave behind.

A little girl taps him on the shoulder. She isn't a Blue Team member. Daniel has never seen her before. This girl is overweight and wears a wide grin below massive bifocals, the glasses wrapping around her head and fastened to her ears by a black safety band. A constant gale of wind rips through the bus and slaps the girl's pigtails against her face.

"How does a lighthouse work?" she asks.

"What do you mean?"

"I mean, how does a lighthouse work?"

Daniel clicks his tongue. "I think the fat guy in the hat explained that already. You should've paid attention."

"No," she says and giggles. "I don't mean that. I mean, *why* does a lighthouse work?"

Daniel clears his throat and turns back around. He stares over to where Todd's face has gone calm and angelic in drowsiness. Through the windshield the bleached-white highway whirs beneath the vehicle.

The girl won't leave him alone. She stands up in her seat and moves her face very close, her breath warm against his ear, loose strands of her hair tickling at his cheek. "Why does a lighthouse work?" she asks again.

He reaches into his pocket. He feels at the plastic bottle, weightless in his palm. The girl's question seems like the most bizarre thing he's ever been asked and it takes him a while to consider the division between *how* and *why*, the difference in what is being asked when those words are changed. This doesn't seem to help him devise an answer, not at first. So Daniel takes one last look through the window before he closes his eyes and waits inside that darkness, waits, waits for a perfect globular speck to appear somewhere in front of him, no matter how distant.

HORTICULTURE

THE MCGUTCHEON HOUSE had been on the market for twenty-one months, something that'd initially concerned Karen and Wes, the young couple who lived in the rambler next door and who, before Bob and Frieda McGutcheon had died—first Frieda, of a sudden embolism, then her husband, three weeks later, from a lack of will to keep going—had attended a dinner party at their elderly neighbors' and had spent weeks afterward remarking to their friends just how pristine the property was, and how lovely the McGutcheons were, and what a shame it was people of their (Karen and Wes's) generation no longer held dinner parties. After a year passed, however, Wes and Karen had learned to relax, to laugh about the old house's misery, even if its untenanted status portended bad news about their own property value, the neighborhood, the real estate climate in the Ashville–Davidson–Murfreesboro–Franklin, Tennessee Metropolitan Statistical Area.

It was Wes who'd bought the bottle of champagne for the house. A Charles Heidsieck vintage. "We'll pop the cork when the place hits two years unowned," he told Karen. They laughed, waited somewhat eagerly for the anniversary.

So it was something of a downer when, in its twenty-second month of listing, the sign disappeared and, on a Saturday in early spring, a moving van rumbled down the street and parked at the curb.

Wes spent that morning watching from the living room. He stood near the windows with a cup of coffee. "You got to see these people."

Karen parted the curtains. Outside, a burly woman was carrying a box to the garage, a cigarette dangling from her lips. "Do you see the man?" Wes asked. Karen waited. After a while the man came around the side of the van. His legs were as thin as a deer's and shot out sideways at the knees. It was difficult to watch him move.

"He's been sitting in the yard most of the time, with those legs wrapped under him. I just saw him get up." Wes looked out again. The woman reappeared, her face bright and slick with sweat. She paused in the driveway and coughed and spit into the yard. "Those legs!" Wes said. "How bizarre."

Karen wanted to say something to Wes, admonish him. What was so bizarre about a disability? The truth was that Wes had been making remarks like this—unnerving remarks—more often. Or maybe he'd always been flappable. When they'd first started dating in college, Karen had thought she'd fallen in love with an artist, a screenwriter. Wes wanted to go into TV; he sat at home, then, in a robe and worked on treatments. "How about this?" he'd yell in the middle of the night, waking Karen. "This guy owns a bar but at night solves crimes..." But that had only lasted so long. After they were married, Wes cut his hair short, and his interest in plot lines was supplanted with an interest in municipal bonds, a Roth IRA.

The man, the new neighbor, went to the back of the truck. His wife handed him an armful of clothes wrapped in a Hefty bag with the hooks of their coat hangers sticking through the top. He struggled up the driveway and into the garage. When he came back out again he looked tired and out of breath. He sat down in the yard. He said something to his wife. He watched her haul more boxes.

Karen felt sorry for him.

She said, "We should invite them over."

Wes chuckled.

"I'm serious. Go over there and invite them for cocktails."

She watched Wes cross the lawn.

—

But the new neighbors didn't drink. The pitcher of margaritas Karen had made sat in the middle of the kitchen table, sweating.

Carl and Regina, the new neighbors, were much older, and polite. Carl apologized about the margaritas. He then began to tell Wes how he and Regina had met in Alcoholics Anonymous. "I'd been a cop," he said. "This was back in Ohio. I was a no-good cop, one of the 'bad ones' you always hear about. That was me."

Regina squeezed his hand. Hers were much bigger, Karen noticed, and rough-looking, the way Karen's father's, who'd been a plumber, had looked.

Carl said, "At first I didn't drink on the job. Respect for the badge and all that jazz. Then, after my first wife left me, I started drinking all the time." He told Karen and Wes how he'd head-onned a pickup and flipped his cruiser into a ditch. "That's what happened to the old knees." He slapped them. "Not worth a tinker's dam."

Before Karen could change the subject, Regina began her own tale. "I was bored, and married to a real son of a gun. But my babies are just peaches. Aren't they, Carl? Carl? Aren't my two babies real peaches?"

"They're peaches, Reggie."

"I drank because I was unhappy, you see." She shook her head. "I lost custody. That's what did it. That's when I knew I had a problem. It always takes something, you know?"

Carl and Regina fell in love during their meetings. They moved from Ohio, hoping for a change.

Karen refilled their tea glasses. Wes began to tell them a story from his office. But midway through, Regina took out a cigarette and lit it and blew a thick cloud of smoke above the table, where it settled around the light fixture. The move stopped Wes in his tracks. A second or two passed, Wes's mouth open. Regina nodded. Finally, Wes began again, though the story had lost its purpose.

After they left, Karen found every scented candle she owned and began lighting them and placing them around the kitchen.

Wes said, "Can you believe that?" He was pacing. "Just lit up. In our home."

"It shocked me, too. But we should give her the benefit of—"

"And did they say one word about our house? No 'Why, this is lovely,' or, 'What a great place you got here.'" Early in the McGutcheon saga, when the house was not selling and neither Wes nor Karen had found the matter amusing, Wes had begun to obsess over real estate websites. He kept the house spotless, as if at any moment somebody would want to evaluate it, judge it. It was no carefree task to live in a home so antiseptic, but Karen hadn't broached the subject. Wes was under a lot of stress from his job. If vacuuming was his way of winding down, well. Things could be worse. "Isn't that just polite?" he was saying now. "Am I wrong here?"

"Give them time," Karen said.

"I was right about them. I knew as soon as I saw them. They're low, Karen."

"That's a terrible thing to say." Karen placed her arms around his waist. "Calm down." She kissed him. Wes settled, though Karen could feel his heart racing.

Of all the chores that soothed Wes, there were none better than gardening. He woke on Sundays filled with a sense of rebirth. He tied his old, grass-stained Asics and was weed-eating by sunrise.

Karen usually joined him after she'd had coffee and a chance to read the paper. Then, the work would begin. The couple would mow and trim hedges. They'd tug weeds and spray ant mounds. They'd clip fresh flowers for the kitchen. They'd prune. They'd edge. They'd dig and plant bulbs. They'd mulch.

Once Wes asked her, while eyeing a hibiscus he'd just planted, "Do you ever feel high out here?"

"I'm sorry," she said, "high?"

"Stoned. Like the soil is making you stoned."

She thought it over. She wasn't sure she understood the question. "I think so," she said.

Wes glared at her. He took off his gloves. "Never mind," he said.

They'd looked at nearly a dozen neighborhoods before this one, and had thought they'd found something north of the city. The trip here was almost out of courtesy to their agent. Karen wasn't necessarily impressed by what she saw. Toward the end of the afternoon, at the edge of a cul-de-sac, Wes had shouted, "Stop the car. Stop right here."

He got out and stood in front of a pinkish house with white trim. Karen followed. The house was not for sale, and even if it were it was not the kind of place Karen would want to live in. But it wasn't the house that'd caught Wes's attention. It was the lawn. The grass was as green as the surface of a lake; they'd planted violas and bearded irises and four-nerve daises. A row of photinia flanked the walkway, and a strong magnolia stood in full bloom in the center of the yard. But what had caught Wes's eye, he told Karen later, was a giant burning bush, a vibrant red Karen had never seen before. A sign was staked in the middle of it all. *YARD OF THE MONTH.*

"I want that," Wes whispered.

A month later, they'd signed on a rambler a few blocks to the east.

Around five-thirty, Carl and Regina's Subaru pulled into the driveway. Regina smiled and waved from behind the wheel. They came across the yard, Carl holding Regina's arm for support. She had on a navy dress and a pair of hose. Carl wore a tweed jacket. Regina held a Bible.

"Been at it, have you?" Carl said.

Wes nodded and looked over what they'd accomplished that morning. He grinned.

"Don't over-exert yourselves!" Regina said. "It's hot already. Isn't it, Carl? Hot? For this time of year?"

"It's hot."

"We've been looking for a church today," Regina said. "We tried the Methodist place last week but didn't care for the sermon." She smiled and waited, as if expecting a recommendation.

"Well," Wes said, finally. "There are a lot to choose from."

Carl said, "Arrrggh!"

"It's his knees," Regina said. "He can't stand for long. Do you want me to take you inside, Carl?"

"No, no," he said. "I'll just take a seat. Help me down, will you?"

Regina helped him onto the grass. Carl stretched his legs out as best he could, leaned into the St. Augustine. They continued the conversation—Regina complained of the hassles of forwarding your mail—but it was a strange thing, Karen thought, to talk to a grown man while he sat at your feet.

It grew dark. Regina helped Carl to stand. Karen watched them struggle back to their home and disappear inside.

She told Wes to get showered. It was dinnertime. She grabbed his wrist, but he wouldn't move.

"What is it?" she said.

Wes pointed at the grass, to an imprint Carl's body had made in the sod.

It is a desire to get it right, Karen thought, watching Wes wash the dishes and re-press his tie for work. If he were to spill coffee on *The Tennessean*, he would stop to buy a fresh copy. Karen knows he grew up an army brat; by the time he was twelve he'd lived in no less than nine places. He believes in homeownership, Karen thought.

June. The heat deepened. Karen and Wes worked hard to keep their flowerbeds watered. Carl and Regina's yard was another matter. Their holly bushes had not been pruned since they'd moved in, and branches reached into the walkway. And when Wes mowed, the contrast between the two lawns was made even more startling. On their way home from dinner or a movie, Wes often slowed the car in front of the McGutcheon place and sucked his teeth.

Karen noticed Wes eyeing his neighbors, obsessing over their property. He was waiting to see if either of them would come out into the yard carrying hedge clippers. But on Sundays, they went to church.

—

One afternoon Karen came home to find Wes sitting in a chair in the dining room, drinking the Heidsieck. The lights were off. Wes had his eyes fixed on the window. Before Karen could say anything, Wes said, "Have you seen the HOA letters piled on their porch? It's as if they don't even care." He picked up the champagne bottle, poured the last of it into a coffee mug.

"Carl is disabled, honey. And Regina—"

"Then they should hire somebody." Wes stood. "It'd cost them a hell of a lot less than the fines they're about to receive."

Karen moved to him, took the mug from his hand. "We could help them," she said.

Wes scoffed. "Help them?"

"Sure. We could run the mower over their lawn while we're out there. A little pruning, trimming."

She expected Wes to laugh. For free? she thought he'd say. Instead, his eyes lit up. "It wouldn't take much," he said. "Not with both of us."

"Maybe only an hour. What's another hour?"

"That's a great idea," Wes said. "Jesus, that's perfect."

He reached for the coffee mug. Karen pulled away. She put it to her lips. The champagne was too sweet.

They were nervous about approaching the subject. Regina brought a casserole and, after dinner, Wes fumbled through the proposal. Karen watched him. She knew he was doing his best to be polite. Her husband, she understood, was not a gentle man.

To her surprise, Carl and Regina didn't hesitate to accept. Carl let out a chugging bout of hissing laughter and moved close to Wes and took up his hand and said, "This is pure heartsong, right here. This is just something from the heart."

Regina embraced Karen. When she pulled a cigarette from her purse, Wes suggested they move the party out onto the deck, to enjoy the beautiful summer night.

Karen felt her anxiety lessen. She felt the warmth of a night spent with old pals. And Wes looked at ease, happy.

Carl was wearing shorts. Karen snuck a look at his legs. Hairless and thin, but his feet were normal-sized. They looked massive by comparison.

—

Before he came home from work that Friday, Wes stopped by the nursery and bought a few shrubs to plant in Carl and Regina's yard. When Karen told him she didn't want to spend money on the project, Wes said, "I'm with you, honey. It's just that their yard has serious potential."

They mowed. They trimmed hedges. They tugged weeds and sprayed ant mounds. They clipped fresh flowers for the kitchen. They pruned. They edged. They dug and planted bulbs. They mulched.

Then, they did it all again.

The next weekend, Wes came home with a Bradford pear sapling. It hung over the tailgate of this truck. "Don't worry about the money," he told Karen. "I've got it under control."

They spent entire weekends gardening. Wes worked with a determination Karen had never seen before. He skipped lunches. By nightfall he could do little more than shower and fall asleep.

One afternoon, Karen quit early and went inside and bathed and read a magazine. When six o'clock came and Wes still hadn't come in, she began to worry.

She found him over in the neighbor's flowerbed, talking to a perennial he'd just planted. "This is it, my friend," she heard him mumble. "Your own little piece of the world. And it's a good one, too, so I hope you remember how goddamn fucking fortunate you are to have it."

That night, he collapsed from heatstroke.

"Enough," Karen said the next evening. "We're done." Wes had taken the day off work to recover. He was lying on the couch, a blanket over him. He said he understood. He told her he agreed, wholeheartedly.

But the following weekend, Karen woke to an empty bed. She put on her robe and went outside and saw Wes dragging the mower across Carl and Regina's yard. He waved to her, smiled.

Now it is mid-July. Beneath clear, deep skies and a wide sun, children ride their bicycles. The community pool is always full. From their front stoop, Karen and Wes can hear the trill of the lifeguard's whistle.

It is Wes's idea to plant a burning bush. When he told Karen, she said nothing, only nodded. What's the use? All she hopes now is to lend a hand. The sooner it is planted, the sooner they can be done.

It takes the couple all afternoon. They have to cut through hard clay to dig a hole wide enough for the bulb.

Carl and Regina's sedan pulls into the driveway.

Regina says, "Oh, Carl! Will you look at this place? Will you just look at it?"

Carl squirms free of his seatbelt and gazes over his new lawn. His mouth trembles. "A real beaut of a job, friends!" He grabs Wes's hand with both of his.

Wes says, "We planted violas and four-nerve daisies. A Bradford pear. We planted photinia and—"

"Well, it looks wonderful," Regina interrupts.

"Wes mowed in a cross-stitch," Karen says. "The homeowner's association loves that. They will—"

"It looks great," Carl says. "Better than great."

"But we've also put in something special," Wes says. "It's a gift for you." He leads them through the lawn, Carl grunting as he struggles to keep up. Wes points to the new addition and the neighbors look it over for a long time.

"It's called burning bush," Karen says.

"Uh-huh," Carl says.

"It's nothing to look at right now. But wait until its leaves change."

"Then you'll see why it's called that," Karen says.

Carl nods. Regina has a fixed smile on her face, her chin pulled back into her neck.

"Anyway, it's all topnotch, really wonderful," Carl says and sits down in the fresh-cut lawn.

"Who knew?" Regina says. "Who knew we would ever have something like this?"

"Hey," Wes says, grinning. "Maybe you'll win yard of the month."

They do. Carl and Regina. The homeowner's association puts the sign in their lawn. Families in sedans slow to look at the winning lawn.

It is August now. Karen thinks the sun is trying to kill her.

—

"Is that too bloody?" Carl asks. Karen and Wes have been invited to their neighbors' house for a dinner, a thank-you for lending a hand.

"It's fine," Wes says.

"Because I can put it back on the fire. It's no problem for me."

"It's fine."

"You're sure?"

"Yeah, I'm sure."

"Carl can cook a wonderful steak, can't he?" Regina says.

"It's great," Karen says.

"The key is in finding the right cut of meat. A lot of people think a filet is a filet. But it's trickier than that. You have to really hunt for the good stuff."

They are seated in Carl and Regina's backyard, a place neither Karen nor Wes has seen before. The grass back here is dead, scorched by the summer heat. One of the live oaks has anthracnose, Karen notices. The leaves look scorched. The tree will die soon. She notices Wes noticing it, too.

Regina called earlier in the afternoon and told Wes that she and Carl had a gift, something of repayment. Wes fights through dinner—

the meat, the apple juice, the undercooked potatoes. He glances at Karen. It's her job to come up with an excuse for them to leave.

When they're done with the meal, Carl belches, apologizes. He says, "We're so glad to spend the evening with the two of you. I know I speak for Regina when I say we think the world of what you've done for us, think the world of you as our neighbors."

Karen and Wes smile.

"When we left Youngstown," Carl says, his voice dropping, his mouth sagging, "we were looking for something. We were looking for a fresh start. To leave our pasts behind." The sun has gone down. Karen can't tell if he's crying or not. He says, "Some cop I was." He chuckles. "You should've seen me back then."

Regina takes over. "What Carl means is that what you've done for us, well—"

"A blessing," Carl says. "A true blessing!"

"It was nothing," Wes tells them.

"It was for us," Regina says and nods and stares at Karen, as if she's trying to see inside her.

Eventually it is too dark to stay outside. Carl and Regina invite them inside for coffee. They insist.

The house smells like cigarettes. The furniture is worn. Karen thinks the people who drive by this house to stare at the lawn believe Carl and Regina are something they are not. It angers her. And the anger makes her ashamed.

Regina pours coffee and sits next to Carl. His legs are folded under him and to the side. His hair looks wild—curly streaks of silver jutting away from his scalp. His glasses are dirty.

"We want to share something with you," Carl says.

"No, Carl. Not *share*."

"What's wrong with share?"

"We want to give them a gift. It's a gift."

"Fine," Carl mumbles. "You do it."

Wes and Karen scoot forward on the couch, put their elbows on their knees and wait. Wes gives a half-smile. Karen watches Regina sip her coffee, place the mug on a coaster. She turns slowly to a side table. She pulls open the drawer.

Carl says, "We've been thinking about this for a long time. I asked Regina, 'Regina? What's the greatest gift we could give our dear pals?' And then we realized."

Regina's hand leaves the drawer, holding a Bible. "It's the gift of everlasting life."

"As payment," Carl says. "As a thank-you for the yard."

"And because we love you. We just love you, Karen. We love you, Wes."

Karen clears her throat. She tries to look past her neighbors and out onto the backyard. She wants to see the dying tree, the way its bare limbs striate against the darkness of the evening. But all she can see is a reflection of the inside; all she can see is herself sitting on a dingy sofa next to her husband, a man who, at this moment, looks like a stranger.

"We want you to know the depth and fullness of life, just like we do."

Wes moves back in the sofa and crosses his legs and puts a hand up to his mouth. "I see," he says.

"We want you to know the Holy Spirit," Carl says.

"To be baptized in the blood of Christ," Regina says.

There is a silence. Wes has to clear it by coughing and leaning forward again.

He says, "Do you have a pamphlet we could take home?"

Carl and Regina give him a smile, a grin that, to Karen, looks to be out of pity. Carl sighs. "No, Wes. We don't have a *pamphlet*. We aren't offering you a *pamphlet*. It's something much bigger, much more important than a *pamphlet*."

Karen feels sick now. She has her eyes on the blackened window. The backs of her neighbors' heads look like two river-washed stones. What she sees, too, out of her periphery, are the massive bare feet of Carl—those enormous, vile feet he has settled on the couch.

Carl says: "The truth is this. You   do   not   know   life. Youjustdon't."

Regina nods.

"I know you think you do. But you don't. You don't know the fullness of it. You've never felt high off, off—"

"Just being alive. Carl. Right?"

"Yes, exactly," Carl says to his wife. "Off just being alive. You've never felt rebirth." Karen can't take another sip of coffee. She nods. She waits for Wes to say something, to get them out of there. But Wes is silent. Wes hasn't moved an inch. Move, Karen thinks. Say something.

And Wes does. Finally, he says, "We try to be good people. We try to give."

"See, but you see—that's great; that's just fine," Carl says. "But it's not about giving. It's not just about giving. Giving is a nice thing, and a good start." He grows quiet; he looks frustrated.

Regina mumbles. Karen can't quite make out what the woman is saying; if she were to guess it'd be something like, "Please, Father. Please, Father."

Carl says, "Let me ask you something. What is it you want? What is it you're after?"

Karen feels now as if the lights from the lamps are giving off intense heat.

Wes chuckles. "That is a weird thing to ask someone."

"Why is it weird?"

"It just is."

"Humor me with an answer."

Karen and Wes look at each other.

Wes says, "We want a neighborhood with very little crime, like this one."

"Nice cars," Karen finds herself saying, though she has never really cared one way or another about cars.

"Yes, but a nice garden, too. We want a nice lawn."

"I think we have that, Wes," Karen says.

"No debt. No financial fears."

Karen says, "Maybe to go to the opera every so often."

"The opera?" Wes says.

Regina says, "Sweet Father."

Karen shrugs. "Or something like that. The museum. The opera. The theater.

"Museum?"

"Anyway, that is sort of what we want," Wes says. "We want a nice house with a nice lawn. We want nice cars. We want to go to the opera, apparently."

Regina has her eyes closed. Carl is staring at them. He nods. He just keeps fucking nodding, Karen thinks. She says, "Why? What is it you want? What *exactly* are you after?"

Carl grins and adjusts his glasses and struggles to stand. Regina is quick to offer to help him, but Carl shoes her away. He moves slowly, painfully, across the living room and stands between Karen and Wes. He looks at them for a long time. Then he moves over so that he is standing directly above Karen. He leans in. He leans in so close Karen can smell the coffee. Carl reaches an arm out and, gently, places a palm on her forehead. "Paradise," he says.

Wes is not in bed. Karen checks the kitchen and the dining room. She checks the office, finds him nowhere. Finally she opens the door leading to the garage. In the light coming from the hallway she sees him there, sitting on an overturned bucket amongst paint cans and tools and boxes of things they have never thrown away; amongst the lawn mower and gas can and weed-whacker; the pruning shears; the deflated footballs and basketballs; the mountain bikes they have never ridden and the Callaways he rarely uses; the fishing rods and tackle; the set of wrenches someone gave them as a wedding gift; the ant and roach and wasp poison; folded lawn chairs and skis. All of it towers around him like a fortress.

"What are you doing out here?"

Wes doesn't turn to look at her. "Did you hear him? Did you hear what he said to us?"

"Listen," Karen says. "You have work in the morning."

"Paradise." Wes shakes his head.

"They're crazy, honey."

"We helped them. And they repaid us with a goddamn lecture. That's what they did. If they wanted to give us a gift, fine. If they didn't want to give us a gift, fine too." Wes begins to stand, stops himself.

"What are you thinking?" Karen asks him, after a while.

"I'm thinking of going over there tonight. Right now, I mean. I'm thinking of carrying this can of gasoline with me. I'm thinking of torching the lawn, Karen. That is what I am thinking."

She doesn't know what to say to this. She tells him to come to bed. But Wes doesn't move. Eventually she closes the door on him. She leaves him amongst their things. What else is there to do? Pretty soon he'll come to bed. It isn't as though he has another option.

BRASS ON OAK, OAK ON MARBLE, MARBLE ON GLASS, GLASS ON STEEL

I.

They lined the walls, floor-to-ceiling, of my father's home office like big game trophies. *Best New Employee, In Honor of Continued Excellence, For Commitment in His Chosen Field, For Exceptional Leadership, For Visionary Leadership, For Leadership and Outstanding Guidance, For Continued Team Building, Leadership Skills, Exceptional Guidance and Continued Excellence in the Field of...*

My father, an archduke of vapid accomplishment.

II.

Glass plaques. White marble plaques. Rosewood plaques with high-tone brass. Black aluminum on American walnut. Alderwood. Red brass plates on smoky, heavy marble. Copper on coated cherry. Mahogany with glass panels. Upright plaques made of inch-thick crystal sitting on three-pound marble bases. Perpetuals. Plaques with gold-dial clocks. Premium acrylic stones—freestanding—with his likeness laser-etched in the strange floating ether of the glass.

III.

Plaque has its etymology in Middle French (*Plaquer*) and Middle Dutch (*Placken*) and Middle High German (*Placke*), and its origins more or less stem from valiant family crests. Coats of armor. But the modern *plaque*, the commemorative award given by an employer to an employee for the sake of recognizing certain achievements or contributions, is a recent phenomenon, one that did not exist before the Industrial Revolution. According to Humanities Professor Emeritus Jens Reichler:

> ...the first documented case of the use of the commemorative plaque as a means by which an employer could offer non-fiscal compensation to a particular employee (thereby eliminating even the tiniest of budget overhead whilst still bolstering morale) occurred in 1902, in Bismarck, North Dakota, at Whalen & Sons Meat Packing Plant, on December 5, a Friday. The recipient, Bruno Moretti, an immigrant...was granted the award...[for his] ability [as safety inspector] to decrease on-the-clock mutilations by 250%. [PHOTO INSET: CAPTION: *Oliver Whalen and Bruno Moretti at the entrance to Whalen & Sons. Bismarck, North Dakota. 1902. Note Moretti's bewildered expression, unsure as to what he has been gifted*] The whereabouts of the award are unknown. It is conceivable that Moretti took the plaque apart and sold the metal for scrap, using the proceeds to buy shoes for his children.*

This might also serve as the first instance of employer-employee unease. I don't mean in the Upton Sinclair, You've-Lost-Both-Thumbs-in-a-Meat-Grinder-and-I-Couldn't-Care-Less Way, or in the existential questioning of one's worth in the face of the ever-grinding gears of market capitalism. I don't wish to conjure the Wobblies, child labor, poor wages, black lung or the two-loom system. I mean a quieter unease, a more abstract sense of mistreatment, of not being

---

* Reichler, Jens. "Reexamining Conferral Procedures of the Early Twentieth Century." *Journal of Approbative History.* 143–169.

appreciated. Plaques are not inexpensive. Your basic brass-on-oak getup runs upwards of seventy-five bucks whereas laser-etched steel on glass, or titanium with even a modest walnut finish flirts with five figures. Millions of employees have felt the same bewilderment as Bruno Moretti; they often express (rarely in public) a wish for the money over the award. Plaques are garish, difficult to haul around. They are aesthetically loathsome. They've become the butt of jokes, much like fruitcake at Christmas.

IV.

But you would never have known this from my father. My father still saw the connection to chivalry.

V.

So when he died and my mother sold them or gave them away or donated them to Goodwill, she had committed a barbarous act. The doctor had given her a high-dose prescription for antidepressants to help her cope with her grief. Venlafarzine, 375 mgs. We're talking serious shit, here. I didn't know about it, then. The plaques. The pills. I was off at college, learning things.

VI.

Then, at Thanksgiving, I went into the office and found the walls bare. He'd smoked cigars, my father, and so the drywall was stained amber except where the awards had hung. Hundreds of 10"x8" rectangles as white as veneer bicuspids, meticulously spaced.

VII.

—Jesus. What happened?

—I couldn't take it, Charlie. All those things staring back at me. I could see your father's face in the brass. Ghostly, you know?

—Mother, listen closely. I need to know what you did with them.

—Scrap metal, baby. Pawn shops. I think your father wouldn't mind, really. He always wanted to believe in reincarnation. Entrenched

Presbyterianism kept him at bay. Is entrenched the correct word? Was your father ever in combat, Charlie? Or am I thinking of another man, a lover, as I had in those days. I was wanted, son. My flanks were tremendous.

—Mother.

—You owe your flanks to my genetic code alone.

—Tell me you kept a ledger, receipts, some documentation.

—Don't be stupid. Was I ever one of those pathetic women who hoarded receipts.

—You had drawers full.

—You're talking about another life, Charlie. A different person.

VIII.

Later that evening I watched her take a ball-peen hammer to the face of a garden structure, a heavy stone frog my father and I bought her one Mother's Day. I was enraged. I wanted to pummel that fraud doctor.

IX.

She came down finally, and was filled with grief and horror.

X.

I took incompletes in my classes and told the girl I'd been seeing that it was possible for passion to take a hiatus, that the kind of love we had was the kind many in this world would kill for, would be willing to give their earthly possessions for. She disagreed.

XI.

(As for her: it wasn't long before she met a veterinarian and married. They live in the country now, from my understanding, where he pulls calves from Herefords and she runs a day-care. It sounds close to heaven.)

—

XII.

Mother and I took to her Pontiac. We drove through town trying to jog her memory. It was cold; a snowstorm was building to the north; low, sooty clouds descended around us. Downtown, a group of retirees were wrapping Christmas lights around lampposts and constructing a nativity scene near the auto parts store. They were having to contend with a nasty wind, and much of the hay for the manger was blowing across the avenue.

XIII.

Our town looks prettier on overcast days. Most of the mills and factories have outsourced their labor; even the company my father worked for—a manufacturer of the least sexy parts of computers: caps locks, power buttons—has downsized its labor force by two-thirds. In the spring and summer the empty buildings suck all joy out of the blooming gardens and poplars.

XIV.

Mother said,
    —This place looks familiar.
    I pulled the car into the parking lot of a busy pawn shop, its neon sign flashing in grand mal style: G-U-I-T-A-R-S G-U-N-S J-E-W-E-R-L-Y G-U-I-T-A-R-S G-U-N-S J-E-W-E-R-L-Y G-U-I-T-A-R-S G-U-N-S J-E-W-E-R-L-Y

XV.

I would like to describe Jed Horatio, the man behind the counter, in a manner that makes him human, dignified, or at the very least average: a man making a living the way the rest of us are. But I am not able to do that.

XVI.

He wore a heavy trench coat that reeked of gasoline, and he looked pleased as punch, his store filled with people hocking their class rings and wedding bands, their mother's mother's cameos. 30.06s. Les Pauls.

Things they'd once held closest to their hearts. Horatio had a thin, uneven mustache. His right hand held five fat fingers. His left was missing, replaced with an old-style hook, something no doubt conned or stolen from a former customer.

I did my best to explain our predicament to Horatio. A dead father, a neurologically imbalanced mother. He listened, his good hand up to his mustache and the blunt end of his hook gently tapping the glass showcase he leaned against, as if he were wanting me to take another look at the impressive array of butterfly knives available.

After a while, Jed Horatio said,

—You're lucky. I still have it in the back. These types of things don't last long. People want them. You'd be surprised. They buy them here, take them home, do a little editing, revising—a little cut and paste—and wouldn't you know it? Suddenly there's their name, suddenly they're top salesman of 1989 or what have you.

Horatio disappeared into a back room. Mother and I waited. The people around us looked desperate. I thought of making this observation to Mother but decided against it. We were desperate.

The award Mother had pawned was a freestanding piece of engraved crystal fashioned in the likeness of a shamrock, sitting on a tortoiseshell base. Jed Horatio used a handcart to roll it toward us. He used a chamois to polish the crystal, and asked us what we thought.

—Perfect, I told him, running my fingers along my father's name. This is fantastic, I said.

Horatio said,

—Great. Asking price is twelve hundred. I'll throw in an *Abs of Steel* DVD box set. You know, for the holidays. We here at The Trading Tipi want our customers to be happy.

—Twelve hundred? You're out of your goddamn mind.

Jed Horatio shrugged and put his good hand inside his jacket and pulled out the loan papers. No, he said. I'm within my goddamn contractual rights, is what I am.

I looked at my mother. She'd begun to cry. The other customers were now staring at us, filled with pity.

—

XVII.

After I'd maxed out three of my credit cards and after we had loaded the award into Mother's backseat, the two of us spent the rest of the afternoon driving in figure eights, down back streets and alleyways. Nothing came to mind.

—I'm sorry, Charlie. Everything's a blur.

XVIII.

I tried to cheer her up. I took her to an old restaurant she liked. We hadn't been there since I was young. The place was under new management and the food was greasy. But the booths were decorated in tinsel and the waitresses wore Santa hats; some of them even donned Rudolph noses. I believe this helped.

XIX.

Toward the last light of the afternoon, Mother said she remembered a scrap yard on the north end of town. We drove out to where the carefully planned neighborhoods and avenues gave way to hills and tall pines, and the neighborhoods were more groupings of old postwars and trailers in cut-out sections of the woods. The scrap yard had no name, so far as I could tell. But it had been a fixture of the town for decades. It sat just off the highway: sprawling, unorganized acres of rust behind a makeshift fence of corrugated steel. I knew the place was owned by a family, and I knew this family was mostly ignored the way families on the outskirts were. But that's all I knew.

XX.

Mister Newton, the owner, met us in the yard. He left the door to the warehouse open, and as I explained the situation to him I could see, just over his shoulder, the low glow of a television inside. Then I realized a woman was in there. She sat on a couch facing the television, holding a baby in her arms. Mister Newton kept running a tongue along his back molars—bulging his cheek—and then I understood that the Newtons lived here, that we had interrupted dinner.

XXI.

When I finished, Mister Newton shook his head slowly. He wasn't wearing a coat and it had begun to snow. He crossed his arms.

—Gosh, he said. That's awful. That's a real awful story.

Inside, the baby had begun to cry. The woman rose from the couch and came out and looked at us and closed the door. We could still hear the baby.

—I wish like hell you'd've told me all of this middle of last week.

—I can pay you. Whatever you think is fair.

—It ain't that. Here, come with me.

We followed Newton along a path cut out of the wreckage. Mountains of car engines and twisted steel towered over us. It was dark now; Newton had brought a flashlight, though the batteries were dying; every so often we stopped to let him slap the light back to life.

We came upon a wide clearing in the middle of which stood a badly rusted ice chest. Newton placed the flashlight near his feet and opened the latch and the stink of old refrigerant rose from within. He pulled out seven wooden slats and handed them to me. Then he took up the light and shone it down into my hands.

—I've already melted down and sold the facades. All that's left are the panels.

I held them in my hands.

—I'm real sorry about this. Can't tell you that enough. You can keep those if you'd like. Don't suppose they're any good to you, though.

Mister Newton's flashlight went out and he hit the butt of it against the icebox's lid for a good while. It wouldn't come back on.

—There you have it. We're without light.

It was dark now and the snow was falling in heavy sheets. For a while the three of us stood without speaking, and the quiet was large and far-reaching. I tucked the seven wooden slats into my jacket.

Newton said,

—Well, listen. If we're going to get out of here, you're going to have to take my hand. Ma'am, maybe you could take mine and your son could take yours. Think I know this place well enough to get us back to your car.

I felt my mother's hand take mine, her palm warm and soft. We followed Newton through the heaps of garbage, the snow crunching beneath our feet and whirling through the scrap metal and falling on our shoulders and hair. None of us spoke. We didn't know where we were headed, though we knew Newton was leading us toward his home.

XXII.

That was years ago. Later, once we'd made it back to the warehouse, Mister Newton invited us to dinner. And later still, I put Mother in a care facility. She's doing fine. We don't talk about the plaques. I have what I have: seven faceless maple planks and a thick, useless hunk of crystal. It's more than some have.

My father's name is Roy F. Turnley.

I don't expect anything, but if you happen to come across something, something you think might be of interest to us, please don't hesitate to contact us. I've included my mother's contact information below:

A SEASON TOO MANY

Mornings

His wife moves toward the honeysuckle vine with a pair of enormous shears. She has been in the garden since daybreak, left him oatmeal on the stove. He watches her from the bay window. In the six weeks since they left Miami, she has spent nearly every morning planting tropical shrubs: brunfelsia and tree ferns and lancepods and orange blossoms. Last week the man at the nursery told her, Those plants won't grow here in Dallas. She drove home and dug deep holes for sabal palms.

At Training Camp

He walks with The Kid to practice, cleats clacking on pavement, sun centered in a sky so blue it's violet. Fans press against the chain-link, screaming for autographs. They hold limited-edition playing cards above their heads. Ball caps and miniature footballs.

The Kid—only twenty-three, only a handful of months out of USC—acts as if this is routine. He smiles. He signs. He kisses.

The Backup tries to remember his first training camp, whether he had this swagger. But five concussions have left only a faded snapshot, a partial memory imprinted with the bad hair and music of 1989. He signs a Shoney's napkin for a two-year-old: *Best wishes in your future endeavors—The Backup.*

At Bob's Steak and Chop

His daughter slouches in boredom, mouth hanging open. The table closest to theirs is shared by a group of Perot execs who've emptied eight bottles of Cain Five, and the girl half-listens to a story one of them tells about a hooker he knows in Little Rock named The Cave.

His wife orders a martini. She looks tired and speaks slowly of the repairs needed to the house, complains about the homeowner's association, the erratic weather, how the women in Dallas put on mascara just to run errands.

She says: I ran into Rebecca Wells at the gas station. She had her hair done and was wearing a tennis bracelet and Bob Mackie perfume. I could smell it over the gasoline. So naturally, I asked her where she was going. And do you know what she told me? Nowhere. *Nowhere*. She was just out, filling the Volvo. Can you believe it?

The Backup grunts, eyes his daughter. She is seventeen now, with a soft face, her mother's face. But she is nearly six-foot-two with a body as broad as a refrigerator. Seventeen now. Smells like sex. He noticed this first in March—the musky residue of a thin-ankled boy. The kid is something of a wannabe rock star with too much hair. The mane would never fit into a Schutt helmet. They met, if he remembers correctly, in orchestra class, and at first The Backup believed the boy was helping her with the French horn.

You'd never see that in Florida, his wife continues. Everyone there has melanoma, sure. But they're *normal*.

She stares at her husband for a moment, sucks on an olive. When the waitress comes, she orders another. The Backup orders a seven-ounce steak and an extra baked potato. Tomorrow is the season opener. He won't play—The Kid has been given the go-ahead—but The Backup is hardened to the dietary ritual: red meat the night before and as many carbohydrates as possible; half a peanut butter sandwich four hours before kickoff; then, water, water, five salt tablets, water.

And they're all married to pilots! his wife says, as if she has been mulling it over. She laughs. She's drunk now. She says, Have you ever noticed that, honey? All of our neighbors wear aviators.

No, I haven't.

He hasn't taken his eyes off his daughter. Sometimes the smell on her is so overpowering he blushes. She seems not to know, or care. Anyway, she has, for the most part, quit talking to him. He chalks it up to her age, to angst. But if he were honest, and there's no easy way to say this, but if he came clean about it, The Backup would have to admit that he has quit trying to reach out to her. His daughter moves through the house like a specter from some past life—Tuscaloosa of the Eighties, when his senior year put him in the running for the Heisman and he and his wife shared a duplex and the deep-night routine of watching *Jim Vandergaarten's Sports Roundup*, tracking win/loss records of pro teams to guess where they'd end up: *If I'm drafted by Detroit, we're going to have to buy new parkas and chains for the tires. If it's Oakland, we could live for a while in that condo your aunt owns.*

There's a picture of him and his daughter as an infant, taken the spring before they left for Cleveland. He sits on a tree stump near the Black Warrior River wearing tight Wranglers and high-top Reeboks and holding the little girl close to his chest, he smiling, and she still burgundy from the womb.

What has happened since then? An ACL tear. The blur of travel, stops in those rustbelt towns where football replaced good food and lovemaking.

The Backup's wife breaks the silence. She says to the girl, Why don't you tell us about your upcoming performance?

The girl shrugs. What's there to tell?

Are you nervous? Excited?

I guess.

The Backup tells her, You'll do fine. When is it again?

A long time from now.

The middle of October, his wife says.

I'm not even thinking about it.

Are you practicing? You've got to practice.

I'm practicing.

Your father will be there, honey.

The Backup nods, grins. He says, I sure will. That's no problem. I'll be there, darling. I wouldn't miss it for the world.

He takes a sip of water and clears his throat and sits up in his chair and proclaims loudly, In fact, I'll be around a lot more. I'll be able to spend time with both of you, just like I've always wanted.

His wife gives him a small smile. His daughter is leaning on the table, eyes on the ceiling. One of the men at the bar shouts, SO SHE SAYS, FOOTJOB? WHO SAID ANYTHING ABOUT A FOOTJOB? and the family is once again drowned in laughter.

It takes him a moment to consider what he has said. Around. Retired. How will that day be, the one in January when he announces he won't be returning for an eighteenth season? The greats hold press conferences, start off with jokes before breaking down, weeping into their Armani ties. Some can't even make out the word. But for him? A blurb in the Sports section. A quick mention on ESPN. They'll flash a list of ten or so players calling it quits, and somewhere in that mix he'll see his own name followed by career stats, numbers pegging his life to a mathematical truth: 2711 Comp; 4242 Att; 63.9 Pct; 29004 Yds; 150 TDs; 134 INTs. Overall Rating: 82.9

Week One

Final minutes of a game that has gone wrong. The Kid has shown his age, his lack of experience. Nervous before kickoff, he drank too much water and vomited on a sound speaker.

He has settled down since, pulled Dallas to within a field goal.

Not much time left. Commercial break. Two-minute warning. When the cameras zip across the guy-wire above the field and focus on the stands, fans jump to their feet and cheer and wave to people at home.

The Backup chews gum with a ball cap twisted backward on his head. He listens to the uproar, fans filled with beer and eight-dollar nachos and dread of tomorrow's commute. The Kid takes the field with the ball at Dallas' thirteen-yard line. He has his work laid out. He's smiling, though—has been since the end of the third quarter. It's taken him only three-fourths of a game to figure out what some players never do: this is the same game you have been playing since you were seven years old, since Pop Warner—since you were six and your helmet weighed so much you couldn't hold your head straight.

The Backup inches toward the sideline. The Offensive Coordinator paces, shouts at wide receivers; he holds his headset in his hand. The referee blows the whistle and the Coordinator turns around and catches eyes with The Backup, raises his brow, moves near him and mumbles: we'll see what this guy's made of.

The Offensive Coordinator paces, shouts at wide receivers; he holds his headset in his hands. But The Backup knows the game belongs to the starter: the way he held himself during commercial break—hands kneading the towel hanging from his waist; eyes on the scoreboard, standing alone at the four-yard dash while his teammates shifted weight, hands on hips, short of breath from excitement. Body language. The game is body language. Or maybe it's like playing bass behind a jazz legend. Or maybe it's more of an improvised dance. Keep with the tempo, go where the game goes; don't think; don't think; feel the rhythm and follow it without pause, without reflection; it's just an uncontrolled pulse, despite steps learned and strategies studied. The game has its own intentions, and once you feel them and fall into the syncopation all there is to do is do; is move. Action only; only action—the body moving; every vein and organ and strand of hair unified: gall bladder, toenail, uvula. You reach this point and the secret schemes devised in meetings come into full view: blitz packages, signals from the bench, headset tête-à-têtes transmitted from above the field; the calls by middle linebackers—*Tango, Tango; Oskie Oh-One, stay on him:* all of this surfaces at once, as clear as the click of the play clock. In black and white. In X and O. The Backup knows this kid knows.

He hits a slant for eight yards. Picks up seven more with a shovel pass. Pump fakes to the left, comes back the other way, then sees a seam in the Cover Two. Ball to midfield. Timeout. Whistle bleats and the stadium is deafening, the hot Texas night falling down through that giant hole in the dome *so God can watch his favorite team, America's Team:*

blue star on silver helmet, yes, sir; that's the team the Most High puts money on, and when he gambles don't you know he don't ever lose. The Kid jogs to the sidelines, grinning. His face gleams with sweat. Short of breath. Grinning. He is there, in the dance. All procedure now. No way to break the pulse.

The Backup smells antiperspirant rising from his shoulder pads.

They're going to bring a weak-side rush, the Coordinator says.

What do you think, bud? The Kid asks The Backup.

Look for the out route. Let the receiver get to the sideline to kill the clock. If they blitz or no one is open, toss the ball through the back of the end zone. Don't take a sack. Don't throw into coverage. Play for the tie if you have to.

The Kid nods, winks. The commercial break ends and the crowd rises like a sheet caught by a breeze.

It took The Backup four years to find the rhythm. He fell in and out of it in Cleveland, in a matter of six plays. Similar situation as tonight. Light snow, though. Winds NNE at 10–12 mph. He completed four in a row before a nose tackle rolled into his leg. Helmet against ligament. When he tried to get up, one of The Backup's teammates shoved him back to the ground, told him to relax, to stay down, man, it don't look too good. Stay down, brother; you're all right, baby. He learned later it was his right guard. In the training room the guard said: your knee went off as loud as a gunshot. Welcome aboard the SS Crippled. The man tapped on his own knee brace. The ACL tear put him out for the rest of off-season and left him with a taste for Lorcet and a six-month trial separation from his wife.

The defense shows blitz.

Blitz! The Backup shouts from the sideline. Blitz!

He should check-off. He should call an audible, shout, *Easy, Easy! Check red eighty-one! Red eighty-one!*, a safe play holding the tight end to block.

Instead he drops back. The Backup pushes his head through between the Coordinator and the punter. He watches a defensive end wrap an arm around The Kid, watches The Kid break free, dodge another tackle and spring toward the line. He rifles a pass into the end zone to the tight end. The pass looks high, but The Backup can't see the outcome. He doesn't have to. The stadium erupts. His teammates leap past him onto the field. The Coordinator tosses his laminated game plan, trots out with his hands raised. The Backup spits out his gum.

Post-Game

He is drunk by midnight. He sits in the living room with his knee up on a sofa pillow and beneath it, a heat pack. Force of habit. There is no pain tonight. The television flashes highlights from the game. The Backup twists a tumbler in his hand, watches The Kid squirm out of danger, fire the ball into the end zone. Smiles and laughter during the press conference. Questions about the future of the team. The Kid says, We can only take it one week at a time.

His wife is in their bedroom. A former neighbor called, a friend of hers, one of the women she used to play cards with. So often he hears his wife's laughter, though most of what she says is muted by the loud thud of music coming from the room above him, his daughter's bedroom, into which the girl has disappeared with her boyfriend.

It is late. It is time for the boy to go home. The Backup has been waiting for his wife to do it, for his wife to go upstairs. He imagines the boy again—the nest of hair, the tight jeans, the shitty, oxidizing car parked catawampus outside the house. The boyfriend never looks him in the eye, has never introduced himself or shaken The Backup's hand. He's never complimented The Backup, never told the man the kinds of things (sure, it'd be bullshit, but what's wrong with bullshit?) he always imagined a boyfriend would say: *Nice to meet you, sir. Yes, sir; I like football. I LOVE football. Gosh, it's such an honor to meet you. I remember that game...* Instead he hides behind his bangs, stands a half-foot behind the girl, waits, as if in painful desire, to disappear upstairs.

He hears his wife say, Everything you'd imagine it to be.

The Backup finishes his drink and pulls away from the couch with a grunt and the cracking of joints. He walks upstairs, the bass of hip-hop thudding down the hallway. He stands outside the girl's bedroom, almost knocks but drops his hand and, instead, presses an ear against the door. He waits. He listens.

In the Garden

His wife has had the St. Augustine torn out. Today it has been replaced with carpet grass. The project is completed.

The Backup stands on the porch and watches his wife amble across the new lawn. Hands on hips and a wide smile, she turns to him and says, Do you know what's missing? A swimming pool. We had one in Miami and used it all the time.

I wish you'd said something before the lawn was re-sodded.

She ignores him. Joining her in the yard, the man has the strange sensation of being in two places at once. She has created an exact replica of their yard in Florida. He wants to say more. He wants to remind her that this is not Miami, even with a pool. A pool will be useless half the year, and the orchids and ferns she had shipped from the coast will freeze, will wilt soon. They will be dead by Thanksgiving. But his wife lets out a long, pleased sigh, and for the first time, standing in the rich green grass, she looks at home.

With a Neighbor

He meets Martin Wells at the edge of the pond. Martin's house abuts the water directly across from The Backup's property line. Each Monday the two men take to the jogging trails that run between their houses and through the hills of the neighborhood, past the tennis courts and public pools and that, finally, jut away from the streets and cul-de-sacs and disappear into a thick copse of sumac and briar and rabbit grass.

The knee brace clicks every time The Backup's sole hits asphalt. Three miles in and tendonitis flares.

How do you like the neighborhood? Martin asks.

Click. Click. Click.

I like it. It's taking my wife longer to adjust. She thought we were staying in Miami for good. She thought last season was the end of the road. We lived in a neighborhood where all the mailboxes looked like tiny houses. We knew the mailman by his first name. The women played Bunko every Thursday night, and even our dogs were all friends. She cried when I told her I'd been traded.

Why didn't you just retire?

The Backup shrugs, says, The money was good. Plus, I thought I'd have a shot at starting here.

The answer is the best he can think of, though he knows immediately it isn't true. He could tell Martin he thought the trade would do him good. He could say he is worried the game is his iron lung, the only thing keeping him alive, or that some nights he gets out of bed and sits in the living room unable to sleep, terrified of his own home, worried that, once the constant travel has ended, he will be left with a kind of reverse motion sickness, the calm proving his bearings are shot to hell.

Click. Click. Click.

Wells says, I hear that. TransAtlantica wanted to move us to Chicago. Rebecca had a fit, said she couldn't stand to move. I ended up taking a worse contract. But we're happy. We are where we want to be.

The Backup slows.

Click. Click. Click.

The muscles in his thigh constrict. Can we take a breather? The Backup puts his hands above his head. Sooty clouds move in quickly from the north. The sun disappears.

Aw, shit. Getting old sucks.

Martin chuckles, wipes his brow. Wells is a short man, balding, with rings of silver hair around a steeple of pink flesh. The Backup suddenly realizes his neighbor is older than he, perhaps by as much as a decade.

You know, Wells says, we're hosting a neighborhood party in two weeks. Anyway, if your wife is having a hard time with the change—if she wants to make friends—the two of you are more than welcome.

The Backup nods, spits again. His breath returns but the pain in his knee comes in currents. The spot where facemask met joint aches in the cooling air. Okay, he says. Yeah. Count us in.

Week Nine; Or, In Kansas City
Third quarter. The Chiefs rush seven and The Kid's thumb catches between two helmets and splinters at the middle knuckle. He doesn't tell the trainers, doesn't come out of the game. Dallas loses, and by the time the players have made it to the locker room, the thumb has swollen and is discolored. It looks like a giant slug. Coaches tell The Backup to prepare for Washington.

Preparation
He skips his daughter's performance. He tells her he has to study the playbook. He says, Washington runs a complicated defense. Blitz packages called off at the last second, zones, sometimes no down-linemen.

She nods, says, Okay, Daddy, she says. Says it without emotion, as if he'd just told her he was running to Home Depot. He waits a moment in the doorway and when she says nothing else, he raps his knuckles against the jamb and leaves.

He sits in his media room, watching film from the prior week. He looks for patterns, for pantomiming signals coming from the safety. He looks for body language. The pond between his house and Martin's shimmers black through the darkened windows. Stars reflect on the water's smooth surface. Martin's house is dark and The Backup's is quiet and the only noise is a slight breeze running through the tops of the trees.

Studying for a game was something he used to do with his wife. Their duplex was not far from Bryant-Denny Stadium, and he would walk home after games and find her sitting cross-legged on the carpet, drinking cheap beer and rifling through a worn composition notebook she used to track his statistics. Every completion, every down, every snap. She was his best critic. They fell in love dissecting SEC defenses on shag carpeting.

The Backup hears her Saab pull into the driveway. The engine turns off. He listens to domestic sounds: cabinets banging, kitchen chairs grating against wooden floors. Later, footsteps thud up and down the stairs. Bedroom doors slam. Showers run. Televisions blare. Then, quiet. It's one-thirty in the morning.

He slips out into the backyard. The jagged shadows of the tropical plants reach toward him. He walks down to the edge of the pond and puts his hands in his pockets. They are 15.2 miles north of the airport. Sometimes the 747s fly so low he swears he can smell jet fuel in the air.

At 35,500 Feet

When the clouds thin, he sees the twinkling lights of some American city—some place, God knows, he has been before.

At RFK Stadium

He takes his time suiting up: jockstrap; undershirt; knee brace; pants with thigh and knee pads; ankle braces; socks; cleats; cleat tape; rib vest; shoulder harness; back plate; shoulder pads; elbow brace; wrist coach; wrist tape; wedding band tape; eyeblack; helmet; chinstrap; mouth guard. It's a chore to walk through the bowels of the stadium.

Twenty degrees colder in D.C. The crowd is already riled. Cowboys and Indians. The Backup stands in the tunnel next to police officers, shifting his weight from one leg to the other. He listens to the noise of the sixty-five thousand crammed into the stadium. When his name is called, he jogs out onto the field, feeling as if he has just stepped inside a giant hornet's nest.

Washington gets the ball first and makes a good drive out of it. They settle for a field goal.

Commercial break.

The Backup tries to keep warm, tosses the ball on the sidelines. A cameraman zeroes in on him, waits for his cue. The fans near the sideline call him motherfucker and old-ass man. He's heard it before. The taunting doesn't faze him, though he's never been able to block it out completely. These are other grown men, strangers—CPAs and foremen and chiropractors and paralegals—praying for his bodily injury.

He takes the field beneath a harmony of boos. He turns to the head referee, says, Hey, Bruce, let me know when we're back from commercial.

The man looks down at his watch and says, Forty seconds. I'll blow the whistle when we mark the ball.

The Backup nods, cups his hands and blows into them. The referee takes a final look at his watch and sets the ball. Then, just before he places the whistle in his mouth, he puts a palm on The Backup's rear end and mumbles, Good luck to you, bud. I've always liked watching you work.

On only the second play, Dallas' running back breaks through and goes thirty-eight yards, finally tackled at the eighteen. The crowd quiets and The Backup high-fives the offensive line.

They break the huddle and come to the ball in an offset-I. The Backup reads coverage, calls a hot route, raises his palm against the center's groin. The ball jolts into his hands. He fakes a hand-off and rolls a little to the right, side-arms a pass to the slot receiver. The ball rattles against the receiver's chest before he pulls it in, breaks a tackle, crosses the goal line. The Backup pumps his fist and jogs to the sidelines. He takes off his helmet and grins for the camera.

His second drive is equally effective, though an offsides penalty forces the team to settle for a field goal. By the end of the quarter, they lead ten to three.

It doesn't last. Washington is quick to score, and whatever rhythm The Backup has found quickly dissolves after he misreads a zone blitz and is blindsided by a linebacker. The ball pops out of his hand. Washington recovers. The linebacker says, Stay down, cutie pie. Brother, it's going to be a long night for you. He watches the mistake on the JumboTron. He walks off the field, throws his helmet at the place-kicker's net. Halftime approaches. Washington scores again. Someone in the crowd throws a beer at him, is escorted out of the stands to applause.

He knows it's his body. His mind is working all right. He can see who is where, what's coming. But his arm follows a fraction of a second later.

Swarmed by a half-dozen trainers, The Kid disappears into the tunnel and emerges ten minutes later without the metal stint. Instead, fingers and wrist are heavily taped. They've given him a cortisone shot.

The Backup notices the Coordinator speaking quietly to a trainer. The Kid's knitted cap has been replaced with a helmet. Snow flurries spin in front of the gigawatt bulbs. The Backup is told he did just fine; he's told to keep loose, that they might need him again.

He spends the rest of the game on the sidelines, trying to keep warm. Same fans heckling him. Dallas loses, though the broken finger plays no role. After the game The Kid tells a reporter, We just have to prepare better for next week and hope the outcome is different.

At Dallas-Fort Worth International
His wife stands near baggage claim. She has her keys dangling from her hand, arms crossed. He waves and grabs his suitcase and meets her with a kiss. They leave LBJ in silence and cut across lanes of traffic for their exit home. She doesn't mention the game. She tells him the orange blossoms have fallen from the tree, and some of the palm fronds are browning. She says she met with a pool company. They'll be back next week with an estimate. She tells him about the orchestra performance. She says, Your daughter stole the show.

Was she upset?

She doesn't respond.

I'll apologize.

The glare of streetlights whips across her face. She says, I went to Neiman Marcus today and bought you a new jacket. It's more autumnal than anything you own. For the party at the Wells'.

Shit. I forgot about that.

The Backup leans into the leather seat and yawns. Only played one half and he can feel his muscles as tight as coils, ready to spring.

He is sore by the time they reach the house. He decides to change into his pajamas and robe before visiting his daughter. He sits down to unlace his shoes.

The Backup falls asleep sitting upright at the edge of his bed.

At the Party

He wears the new blazer, a burgundy hound's-tooth, with dark slacks and boat shoes. No socks. He and his wife walk along the pond and to the party. Rebecca Wells meets them with hugs and guides them to the kitchen, where ice chests of beer stand open on the floor. The Backup grabs a bottle and moves into the backyard. Men sit on patio furniture, chuckling and rocking in deck chairs.

Martin Wells shakes his hand and introduces him to the rest. His wife was right. All of them are pilots. Jimmy Slocum flies for Northwest, and Chuck Brennan is with Delta. Erik Montgomery and Junior Wright are both with American. Lee Henrietta pilots a private jet for a real estate mogul.

Wells says, We're glad to have a non-pilot on the block. Finally we can talk about something besides wind shear and holding patterns.

The Backup sits on a chaise longue. Nobody speaks. The men stare at him, skeptical he's the same man they saw on Fox last Sunday.

Chuck Brennan breaks the silence. So, he says, what's it really like to play pro-ball? I mean, what does it feel like when you've got a heavy rush coming at you?

The Backup drinks half of his beer in one long swig. He tells them, It probably feels like getting an airplane up to full throttle and then tossing the yoke out the window.

They laugh. Jimmy Slocum says, We saw that hit you took in Washington.

Martin whistles and shakes his head.

Junior Wright asks, Did that hurt?

Lee Henrietta says, *Did that hurt?* What kind of a question is that?

Erik Montgomery says, The guy wasn't going in for a hug.

Brennan says, And he's a pro-bowler. Won the Nagurski Trophy in college.

Actually, The Backup says, it doesn't hurt, not until the next morning. When you're out there, you don't feel much of anything. But a hit like that, coming from a player like that. The next morning, it's a bitch just to take a leak.

The men laugh, then Lee says, Tough loss.

You did what you could, Martin Wells says.

Oh, sure, Brennan says. The outcome was about what we expected. Don't take that the wrong way, he says. I mean, we were all cheering for you, hoping for the best.

The Backup glares at him. Lee Henrietta says, At least it wasn't like in Cleveland. At least he didn't go low on you.

Lee has a red face, a drunk's leathery skin. His bloated stomach is forced into a polo shirt. He holds a thin, unlit cigar and a tumbler rim-filled with bourbon. He says, It's all right! All you've got to do now is pray to the sweet Lord that The Kid doesn't get injured again.

Chuck Brennan says, Lay off, Lee.

Montgomery says, Lee's had one too many. When he has one too many, he likes to give people a hard time. He thinks it's funny to give people shit. It's the reason he doesn't have many friends.

Lee says, Except these assholes! They're pansy enough to put up with my mouth. No, but they're right. That's true about me. Anyway, I'm sure you're used to it. I mean, my God, that team you had in Miami. What a disaster. He chuckles, says, That wasn't your fault. You had a bunch of morons for teammates. Still, for a million in signing bonuses, I think even I could score every now and then. Henrietta lets out another guttural laugh.

The Backup smiles. He says, I don't see how it's any different than flying a plane. I mean, what do you guys *do*, anyway? Press a few buttons and try not to hit the side of a mountain?

The pilots rock in their chairs. They finish their drinks quickly. Lee seems to be the only one smiling. He says, Okay. I can take it. I'll take that and dish it right back out. Even with this gout, even with this gout here in my left leg, I could've picked you off eighteen times the other night.

You want to give it a try?

The men glance at each other. The Backup stands and takes off his sports coat and drapes it over the back of a lounge chair.

Give it a try?

Marty, you've got a football around here somewhere, right?

In the garage, Marty says.

Get it. And pump it up, too. Don't give me a fucking loofah to toss around.

The men follow him into the front yard and stand beneath the streetlamp. Martin comes out of the garage with the ball. The Backup puts his hands up, whistles, and Martin lobs a wimpy, crooked pass.

He says, Here's how it works: I want Erik and Martin and Junior. Jimmy and Chuck are on defense. Lee, you are too.

The pilots are motionless. He eyes them. He slaps the ball. He says, Well? Are we going to play or are we going to look at one another and pick our asses?

It's a game of two-below. The Backup huddles his offense and gives them directions. A hook and lateral. A pump-n-go. A play-action fade. Against Martin's soft Bermuda, the men relive their younger years, replay what they've seen on television. They sprint, catch, move with the game. Their breath holds in the chilly air. The ball floats through the soft light. It hits them in the back of the head. In the chest. Mumbles of *shit* and *my bad, man*. They lose penny loafers and wallets. They keep going, keep reaching toward fantasy pylons and first-down chains. The Backup scores five touchdowns before the women come out onto the sidewalk. What on earth is this? What are y'all doing? They laugh at the mistakes, at these bloated strangers doing impressions of the lean athletic men they married twenty years ago. They sip wine and watch the men gallop in a meaningless game, a bad decision, a choice that'll leave them with nothing but stiff muscles and doctor's appointments. Cries for Icy Hot and Bayer. The Backup's wife stands in the middle with her arms crossed. She gives him a long ugly glare. A scold.

The air comes in through his nostrils and stings his lungs. The ball feels natural in his hand as he huddles his team. He smells the liquor-tainted breath of his neighbors, stares over them to where their opponents stand holding the places that already ache. Only the women are watching, but he feels as though it is more than that.

Let's burn these sons of bitches, he says, using his calloused palm to draw routes. They break the huddle and The Backup hikes the ball and drops back. Erik Montgomery lopes along the rosebushes, but it's Martin Wells he zeroes in on. Martin is open. The Backup plants, fires a spiral into the end zone. The ball hits Wells in the hands with a loud thud, ricochets, floats above his head and into the arms of Lee Henrietta.

Lee pauses in disbelief. He looks down at the ball as if it'd dropped from another planet. Then he grins and struts past the women, his voice shrill and pocked with laughter. I picked him off! Did you see it, Helen? I picked him off!

Henrietta's plump figure saunters through the light, ball raised in front of him. For a short moment The Backup's eyes lock with his wife's. Then he focuses on Henrietta. Everyone else has sat down—exhausted, drained.

There's a group of holly bushes behind Lee, and already The Backup sees himself knocking the man into them. He sprints toward Henrietta. Henrietta turns and sees him—all six-feet-five inches, all two-hundred-and-thirty-four pounds. Charging. Lee's face sinks. He stops, tightens his body, closes his eyes. The Backup squares his shoulders. A few feet away, he feels his ankle turn in the soft grass, followed by a quick tingle in his leg. A loud click. A noise similar to one his brace would make if he were wearing it.

The Backup pulls away, stops himself from falling into Martin's bushes. Lee walks into the driveway and drops the ball, looking as if he just narrowly avoided being hit head-on by a Greyhound bus.

The Backup grabs his knee and bites his lip. He knows something has gone wrong, though he says nothing. It is Lee's wife, Helen, who speaks first. Are we done, boys? I mean, can we go back inside?

The men congratulate one another and move toward the foyer of the house. The Backup thinks surely someone must've realized what has happened. But Chuck Brennan only slaps him on the shoulder. Good game, man. Don't worry about that last throw. Wells should've had it.

The Backup takes a step and grimaces. He tugs his shirt away from his sticky chest. He acts like he's catching his breath, calming down. He waits. He doesn't move again, not until everyone has disappeared inside.

In the Garden
Behind him the bright lights of Wells' house make the woods look ablaze. He limps through them, each step tougher than the last, leaning on tree trunks for support.

The back door is locked. He moves the length of the house with his hands against the brick. Halfway along, the toe of his loafer catches on a stake one of the sabal palms is tethered to, and his knee gives. He shouts and falls forward onto an air-conditioning unit. He sits for a long while, cupping the throbbing joint between his hands. He can already feel the swelling.

It is quiet now, as quiet as it has been in a long while. The Backup leans against the side of his house and closes his eyes.

He is jolted awake by a noise he first mistakes as a gunshot. The Backup struggles to his feet and limps toward the side of the house, leans again against the wall. From here he can see the boy's battered car. It pangs and ticks and lets out a belch and dies. Then the passenger door opens, and his daughter steps out into the cold. She stands alone for a while, arms wrapped across her chest. For a second The Backup thinks the girl has spotted him, and he moves back into the shadows.

When he peeks out again, he sees that the boy has joined her; he moves his arms around her waist. They kiss. The Backup expects himself to get angry. But the kiss is not crude. Just a quick moment shared by two people who are young, who believe they are onto something no one else has ever been lucky enough to know.

He hears a sound from behind him and turns to see his wife carrying his burgundy jacket. She stops in the middle of the yard, looking for him. But The Backup says nothing. He leans all of his weight against the house and peeks out toward the street. He hears the couple talking.

Honey? his wife says. Honey, are you out here?

The Backup doesn't respond. He wants to hear what the boy is saying to his daughter. He tries to hobble closer, close enough to make out the words. And though the pain is tremendous and the stress on the joint is causing the injury to worsen, he knows this is something he cannot miss. He forces himself to the edge of the house and cranes his neck as far as possible. And just as he hears his daughter laugh and begin to tell the boy something, a jet plane cuts above them, flies directly over the house, the pond, the garden—low enough to drown out any sound down here on earth.

ACKNOWLEDGEMENTS

Thank you to the editors and writers who helped these stories see daylight: Michael Czyzniejewski and Anthony Doerr, who chose my first short story for publication; to David Daley, Jacob White, J. Allyn Rosser, Mike Ingram and Tom McAllister and Dave Housley; to Sean Bishop and Edward Mullany; to Jensen Beach, Lance Cleland, Dani Shapiro, John Kulka and Natalie Danford.

I am indebted to the entire MFA faculty and staff at the University of Houston, specifically to Chitra Banerjee Divakaruni, Alexander M. Parsons, and Antonya Nelson. I am also grateful for all those who taught me the craft along the way: Peter Turchi, Karen Brennan, John Weir, Wells Tower, Kevin Grauke, John Tait. And to Cheryl Clements, the first creative writing instructor I had.

Thanks to Inprint and to the National Endowment for the Arts for their crucial support.

Thanks to Barry Hannah, whom I met only once and never studied with but who taught me—and many of us—what magic lies within a simple English sentence.

To Mom, Dad, and Allie for giving me an unshakeable foundation. My grandmother, the avid reader. To Lisa, Reed, and Tommy—my family.

And thanks to all my friends and colleagues: Laurie Ann Cedilnik and Glenn Shaheen, Johannes Lichtman, Kyle Minor, Billy Longino, John McDermott, Christine Butterworth-McDermott, Michael Sheehan, Michael Martin, Mark Sanders, Daryl Farmer, Bruce Machart and the Exchequer lads, and to KTCK 1310 AM The Ticket in Dallas.

Andrew Brininstool is the recipient of a 2014 National Endowment for the Arts Fellowship in Prose. His work has appeared in *Barrelhouse*, *Five Chapters*, *Third Coast*, the *Tin House* blog, and *Best New American Voices 2010*. His stories have also received the Sherwood Anderson Fiction Award from *Mid-American Review* and the Editors' Prize from */nor*. Born in Santa Fe, New Mexico, Brininstool is a graduate of the MFA program at the University of Houston. He serves as an Assistant Professor in the Creative Writing program at Stephen F. Austin State University.

CPSIA information can be obtained at www.ICGtesting.com
Printed in the USA
LVOW06s2303170915

454646LV00003B/8/P